Diary of the Other Guy

Thanks to Mumsy and Dadsy, and sisters mine.

And to my friends: Gabriel Ross, Wayne Stark, Adam Guarino,

Michael Kuszay, Michael Lucas, Gabriel Vigil, Liz Teixeira and

Nick Woodfin, thank you.


A special thanks to my former Professor Joseph Reynolds and

Tonya Salyerds for their help and support.

# Diary of the Other Guy
## By
Dorian Aaron Xanyn

Dorian Xanyn
2018

Illustrations: 'The Mind of Jack,' by Dorian Xanyn, 'Dick-

Smile,' by Dorian Xanyn

First Printing: 2018

ISBN 978-0-692-06193-0

# Introduction

This is not an important book. After dozens of rewrites and hundreds of revisions and edits I'm not entirely sure that this is even a good book. Friends, professors, beta readers, editors and other writers have assured me that it's entertaining and engaging, (some even praising my cynical humour, style and voice) and maybe that is all it needs to be, serviceable; a book to kill a few hours. And maybe, hopefully, through that my work might become notable, even if it's just a foot-note.

This book, to my recollection, has two origin sources: a conversation with my father and a conversation with my then-friend Stacy. With my dad we were in the midst of a sociological discussion, something that is not entirely uncommon in my family. The conversation dealt with interpersonal relationships and general reactions to hypothetical stimuli: 'if stimuli $X$ befalls person $A$ then reaction $Z$ would occur.' Always wanting to inject some humour into our conversations he would frequently throw out a joke or quotable line that I would incorporate in my personal lexicon. When I brought up the stimulus of 'a cheating wife' we discussed the possible reactions of the husband and my father exclaimed, "They (the husbands) become *Psychotic-Douches*," a term I used once or twice in this book. My father is the inspiration for the humour and the characters mode of reason.

The other conversation that I credit to the inception of my work is that of my former friend Stacy; on Halloween, at the start of our friendship, during my sophomore year at the University of Hartford. Though we had known each other for a few weeks to a month she mainly avoided my company. We were in her car talking about her sudden change of heart and I learned why she initially disliked me. When we first met she was told that I was engaging in relations with a member of our group who had a boyfriend, though true I did not understand why that would affect her opinion of me. She told me that she assumed that I was an asshole; I then told her my perspective of the situation: I was single, I never cheated on a partner, she was a consenting adult, as was I, and I was not a friend of, or really knew, the girls' boyfriend. She took what I said into consideration but remained firm that I was in the wrong, so I asked, "the rumors you heard were 'Dorian is sleeping with this guys' girlfriend,' right?" she agreed, then I asked, "what if I rephrased it to, 'this guys' girlfriend is sleeping with Dorian'?" and her eyes widened, "both statements are true but when you identify one of us as doing the action then suddenly that person is at fault," she gave credit to, and accepted, my argument even if she was reluctant to do so. I thought about this conversation for a while and began writing a short story with that opinion and my fathers' aphorism in mind.

I planned on submitting my short story titled *The Diary of The Other Guy* in the schools literary journal. I had given a copy to one of my professors, who had been published a couple of times, for a critique. A week later, panicked, I saw him waiting for me before class. We walked down the hall and talked, I feared he didn't like it or was offended and would tell me to drop the idea all together. To my surprise he liked the story; he loved the voice and enjoyed both hating and sympathizing with the main character. His main criticism was the length, apparently I had written eight-hundred words too many for it to qualify as a short story. When I asked what I should take out he said, "nothing: expand, add, make it longer and go from there," which brings me to acknowledging this books awkward length. I emailed and submitted several versions to him throughout my junior year and he shared it with other writer and sent both his and their feedback, but over the summer I had lost contact with him just as I passed novella length. For the past few years I have been editing and re-editing, I hope I have polished it well enough to entertain. Thank you.

Diary of the Other Guy

Diary of the Other Guy

'Feeling that I was born for the sex opposite of mine, I have always loved it and done all that I could to make myself loved by it.'

-Giacomo Casanova, l'histoire de ma vie

Diary of the Other Guy

Diary of the Other Guy

Diary of the Other Guy

# New diary: First Entry
## Prologue

**He who walks on Snow, years and years galore, My Childhood**

I am a man of women, born and raised, and to my knowledge all the events that have had the greatest impact to my life have almost always been orchestrated by, or can be attributed to, the fairer sex. To say I'm romantic currently would be laughable but in my heyday, my youth, I guess I must submit to your accusations. From birth, much like the description of Freud, my first love was that of my mother and to a lesser extent my elder sister Anne. Though my father was there for the first few years of my life, he was drained into the background. This is my base.

I still remember my first interaction with girls in a more social situation, pre-K. I wish I had the memory or writing skills to have kept her name but what I do remember are her freckles and straight black hair, our mats were next to each others during naptime. This, of course, was before anybody had heard the term girlfriend, but judging by our familiarity I would say that would have been an accurate description of our relationship. Though hugging was kind of what kids did, or were forced to do, I only felt comfortable hugging her and would give the occasional kiss on the cheek which she would excitedly reciprocate. We would push our mats close together, overlap our blankets and cover our head to make our own world consisting of us and us alone. I still remember that feeling of anxiety I had when I said those dreaded words 'I like you' and even back then I knew my fate was sealed. There's nothing that can be compared to the feeling you get when you hear that those hidden feelings you have are shared, no matter how old you are, even if she accidently pokes you in the eye while trying to touch the tip of your nose as she says it.

I moved after my relationship hit its zenith, my first lip to lip kiss. I was heartbroken but must have gotten over it fairly quickly, you know how kids are. I only say this because by midyear of kindergarten I got my first official girlfriend, at least the first one whose name I can remember, Marie. We kissed everywhere we could, and you know that just tickled the teachers the wrong way, especially the tyrannical misses Lyn. During one of our lessons; we all sitting on the floor, I sat directly in front of my Marie. Once the teacher had turned away, my love pulled me back, resting my head on her lap and assaulted me with kisses. I had nothing to do with this loving attack and any person with a working pair of vizies could see I was innocent but none-the-less Lyn placed the blame entirely on me, I suspect it may have had something to do with my sex. After the verbal thrashing of a lifetime Lyn felt she still needed to drive the message home, make an example out of me, she forced me to sit three kids away from Marie at all times. She would stop at nothing to keep my love and I apart.

We found a way to skate under the teachers' radar, the plastic play house in the courtyard at recess, fifteen minutes of love. Fifteen minutes of privacy. Fifteen minutes of freedom to kiss in peace. In this year of my life we had just finished unpacking at home and my parents wished to celebrate. I walked in on them, when they were still together, in the horrifying bliss of sex. To comfort my now permanently twisted mind my mother put on her nightgown and took me to the living room in an attempt to stop my screaming. She sat me down on the couch and explained that 'when two people are in love they hold each other naked because they have nothing to hide'. Needless to say I took the message to heart. I loved Marie.

Once when we went to our getaway home I explained what my mother had told me and she was down for it. We stripped. Lo and behold the first time I saw a vagina, this peep show only happened once and lasted for about three minutes. Instead of lying down, holding each other and kissing, as we normally did, we sat at opposite ends of the enclosure looking at each other's body: squints, head tilts and guttural noises accompanied by giggling persisted throughout those few minutes before we started to redress. We liked each other but felt that we had done something wrong, which I guess we did by today's standards, but in my day we would have just been labeled curious.

In second grade, I had lost what charisma I had in my earlier incarnations. I felt awkward and inadequate compared to my fellow classmates: my hair was a curly mop, my feet were too big, I was shorter than most of the other boys, I was the only kid in my grade without a dad, we weren't well off, and on occasion I had to wear some of Anne's hand-me-downs. I was only able to talk to girls as friends, I dare not want anything more, there was a strict divide between the two sexes and by disassociating myself with the boys I had already committed treason against mine. So it would have been wise not to alienate my associated group. I did, however, have a crush on this little blonde girl in my class, no matter how much you hide it the feelings will always be there. I was shy by nature but this girl, in particular, I never said a word to, mainly because I couldn't remember her name for the life of me. I learned how to long.

It was this year that I spent a weekend or two a month at my maternal grandfathers. He was a kind man, a Korean vet (I now suspect his sweetness came from a prescription pad), he had interesting stories and funniest jokes, they were dirty so at the time I didn't get them but the way in which he told them made me bust out laughing. Grandad was the one who told me the story of *The Man Who Walks on Snow*. He said it was an old legend, but I have never been able to authenticate it; he claimed that it was told to him by a footless South Korean man in the cot next to his at the army hospital.

The story is fairly short. It follows a general who was as malicious to his enemies as he was kind to his men. If he or his soldiers came across an enemy village, regardless if they posed a threat, he would pillage. He would take prisoners. Not just the men but everyone they could catch: women, children, the elderly, all would be held or held under his blade. He would ask the enemy soldiers which of the civilians were their wives and children, if one refused to say then all the homes would be burned, all the children would be shot, all their women raped and killed. Then the man who refused to tell would be left to the mercy of his surrounding countrymen. If he did point out his family he would be given a choice: who would he want to keep alive, his wife or his children?

Though malicious his actions were utilitarian in nature. His reputation and army protected his home and his people. Necessary evils will always get a pass. Eventually he would

5

cross the line by intercepting a letter to his second in command written by his wife. The general had seen the seconds' wife once before, she was beautiful and he had thought of her many times. The letter was a poem describing the pride her husband inspires in her every day, the love she feels for him and her desire to be with him once again. After reading the letter the general disguised himself as a common soldier and set his horse to their village. The venture to his mans' wife took a day and a half, at the door the general announced that her husband had died fleeing a battle like a coward. In the widow's grief the general took advantage.

As he laid in bed with her he looked outside and saw that it had begun to snow. This was a death sentence for his men who were without supplies; as fast as he could he rode his horse back to his men. He arrived to a silent camp, he shot his horse so they would have some source of nourishment and hoping the loud sound would draw them out. He explored the abandoned area finding his second hung in a tree, intestines pouring out and the character for *monsters* carved into his cheeks. During his excursion, a group of vengeful villagers attacked. They poisoned the guards, killed the rest in their sleep. He was now forced to return to his village on foot. Angered by this realization he took his gun and shot his horse again.

His feet sunk deep into the snow, with every mile, the snow built higher, and the walk became more difficult. As night set and the temperature dropped he realized that he may die, and he accepted it. He hoped for it. Thinking of the many he killed, seeing the terror in their eyes during their last moments again during what he believed to be his he felt was fitting. A shiver came on and he thought of his second, '*he was a good man*' he thought. The generals' heart pounded softer and softer, his stomach became hollow. The thought of his second, his friend, being mutilated sickened him. He hoped for death again. Suddenly the trek became easier, the snow ceased falling on him, and he began to feel warm. He looked down and to his surprise he was no longer knee deep in ice, he was standing on top of it. There was no change in the color or density or even the look. The general could see that the snow was still falling around him but not on him and a path emerged where the snow would not fall. He followed the mystical road throughout the night and into the day.

Near the end of his journey he saw that the trail led away from his village. He stood half a mile from the sanctuary, not sure whether to continue with the path or risk the elements. He was tired, ready collapse at any moment and he needed some time to think. He looked at his homeland and looked at where the trail went. Still unsure of what to do he sat and meditated for hours. From the village a boy emerged staring at him, from the outskirts the general watched the boy. The brutal general took one deep breath, stood, turned away and continued on the trail. He made his final choice. My Grandad told me this story three or four times when I was a kid, so I'm sorry if I got the details a little messed up.

I spent the remainder of my elementary and middle school years trying to get the attention of the girls around. It was in sixth grade I noticed the girl sitting next to me in math, I thought she was the most beautiful creature on earth, her name was Hannah. Her natural look was better than most girls who were just becoming familiar with makeup. I asked her to the first dance of the year, she agreed. She had the edgy goth look that I loved. I went to her house once about a week before the dance, I gave her an old brass key in a card that said *to my heart*. Her family seemed nice, her older brother was kind of a prick though, a real emo asshole who did nothing but piss, moan and complain about everything. During that visit, Hannah had brought out a Ouija board and I saw my opportunity to steal a kiss. I don't know if she caught on or not but it really doesn't matter, I got what I wanted.

The dance itself was pretty strange; I had never been in such a social situation before. The dark atmosphere, a large crowd of people and pounding music made me feel uneased. I saw some friends and talked to them a little. There was this one kid, Devan, who would go around picking people up and while I was dancing it seemed as though he was doing it to me every fifteen minutes. He actually picked me up so much that it provoked a fight between Hannah and him, and later she and I. She broke up with me on the phone a few days later, I have no regrets. The rest of middle school was flirting and notes with the girls in my class, no dates but the occasional kiss. What else can I say about my early experiences with pseudo-sexual relationships other than I lost my V-card to a whore around my fourteenth birthday, it was unemotional, very mechanical and I blew my load in ten seconds. I do wish I held out for someone I cared about, maybe I would be a better man than I am now.

My first serious relationship that encompassed both an emotional and sexual paradigm came around six or seven months after I became a man with some other little goth number named Jule, she was one year my elder. She was silly, dark and sexy. What sticks in my mind whenever I think of her are those huge sensual lips that glowed like cherries in her bleak complexion, her nicely sized bust for a high schooler and an ass that could fill even the baggiest pair of trip pants. When I first met her she had a beau, but that didn't stop me from flirting, to his dismay she found my presence titillating, my conversation enthralling and put such weight in my opinion. We hung out after school a couple of times a week. We'd watch movies, I gave her dance lessons, and she would complain about her boyfriend. During one of our lessons she started to cry. I stopped the music and told her to sit down. As I held her close listening to the latest fight she had with her boy toy, I looked into her green eyes and asked, 'what if I kissed you right now?' She, sitting in the corner of my dining room, shook her head and said, 'I really wouldn't care anymore,' I did not kiss her that day. I just wanted to test the water. I told her I wouldn't because that would ruin her relationship and our friendship. Yes, I was such a thoughtful young man. They were broken up within a week, and I slid right into position as her new boyfriend.

Jule was the one who got me into bondage. Discovering the bliss of being tied down to my bed, my tongue two inches deep in her cooter while she's jerkin' my gherkin, my hands squeezing that fantastic ass. I found my moment of peace being smothered and having that sour taste rolling in the back of my mouth as I looked down her brown eye in valleys of the great divide. She allowed me to run wild with whatever fantasy I had. There however, like with every relationship, were problems. First, she didn't like my friends. They were all girls and I'm a flirt, so of course that drove her crazy, didn't help that I thought it funny. Second, she was way too ready for a family. Once when she slept over, we woke up early and we, like horny teenagers, started fooling around. I stopped and said 'I'll get a condom,' she said 'no, cum in me. Let's take a chance,' whoa crazy, remember we're just kids. The cracks began to show as time passed, she wanted more, and I was unable to give it to her.

One day while we were going at it particularly hard she asked if we could take a break, she was getting sore. I agreed and was instantly sent into cuddle mode, wrapping my arm around her and started to spoon. I kissed her neck once and she barrel rolled on top of me mounting, I was in shock. 'No,' was the only thing I could get out when she crammed her tongue down my throat and began gyrating. The second I could speak I yelled 'stop!' she chuckled and asked 'why?' while she started thrusting harder. For a moment I thought about it, questioned it and what I came up with was '*I don't know I just don't want it right now,*' but 'I don't want it,' was the only thing I could say. She continued as I turned my head into the pillows and closed my eyes. I tried blocking out what was happening and let my wood drop, as I got soft that wet slapping sound of her cunt smacking against my cock and balls got louder and drew me back in the moment and the stimulation redirected blood back into my member, though from my traumatic perspective it felt like forever the actual assault probably lasted only a few seconds to a minute. She stopped at my whimpering and we instantly got into a fight. She blamed me for everything, for teasing her and then refusing to give it up. And though it may sound crazy I was still in love with her, I tried to make our relationship work, but I couldn't trust her anymore.

A few weeks passed with me trying to make it work with Jule, but I was just terrified to get intimate with her, and she'd get pissed if I refused to sleep with her or even hesitated on the topic. Eventually, she would say 'you aren't emotionally capable of being in a relationship now,' and forced me to break up with her. She wanted it over but didn't want to be viewed as a shallow bitch. Thus began my distrust of the opposite sex for about a year, I hated any girl I didn't already know. This resentment didn't inhibit my appetite; I would play the sad victim whenever one of my gal pals began to get close to me and then I'd seal the deal, this is where I stood, this is where I felt comfortable. I had no obligations, and I could just stop without either party being too damaged. This is but a glimpse in the formation of the other guy. The man built for women.

# Part I

**Michelle Louis Parker, Thursday 9:45am, Safety Time:
Forty-Five Minutes...**

Wake up around 2:30 pm. I'm lying down with my girl
in her bed looking out the window, the leaves rattling in the
breeze, the sidewalk glows white in the summer sun, hot enough
to fry an egg. I can hear Sinatra's '*Summer Wind*' playing in my
head, the sweet feel of nostalgia overcomes me and the annoying
hum of the fan is transformed into a relaxing white noise taking
me to some far away land. Um... sorry about the times not
matching, that might be a bit confusing, I tend to jump around a
lot so stick with me here: it'll all make sense, I promise. 9:45 is
when I arrived at this blonde beauty's place and now at 2:30 our
bodies are pressed together relaxing after our feat of exhaustion.
She's nuzzling her head on my chest; my hand is stroking the
smalls of her back, looking down at her face I'm taking a mental
picture of every bead of sweat on her forehead, those strands of
gold that cross over her eyes, her cheeks and nose are roses.

This place is so fucking hot, the fan is swaying back and
forth making ripples in the mess of clothes that surround us. I
slung my boxers onto the tv at the beginning of our romp for
some comic relief, and they're still there hanging on the edge by
the waistband, out of reach from the fans sway. Michelle is half
out, our hearts are beating in opposition. She's nervous, still. The
tension sustains me, my brain is a flood with chemicals:
dopamine, norepinephrine, serotonin, etc... the lightheadedness
still remains. This is my drug.

I have to put on my skivvies, it's almost time for me to
go.

"Michelle, it's just about time."

"I know," she moves her head slightly lower on my torso
and squeezes me tighter, "a few more minutes."

"Let me put on my panties," she giggles and looks up at
me, "and pants and then I'll lay right back down for a few, ok?"

"Okeydokey," still with that playful smile, at first glance
one would almost mistake that look for innocence.

Walking to the tv to get my underwear, a picture on the
nightstand turned towards the wall catches my eye. I pick it up to
see. It's of her two children a boy and a girl. They are roughly
the same age, but the lass does appear to be the elder one, my

apologies son I know how you must feel. I took my underwear off the tv and put them on. I scan the floor for my pants and get a little sidetracked looking at Michelle's uncovered skinny little figure lying face down in her white sheets and pillows. She looks so peaceful. My pants are under the bed; I walk over, and she rolls on her side, leaning on her arm watching me. She opens her mouth presses her tongue against the inside of her cheek and motions her free hand, imaginary blow job accompanied with a throaty gulping noise. I laugh a little. She then blows me a kiss and quickly rolls over.

On with my pants! And I'm back on the bed cuddling with Michelle. She starts kissing my stomach gently.

"*Si una donna e tranquila, ha bisogno un uomo,*" I whisper.

"What's that?"

"You don't know?"

"Only English... and a little Portuguese. No Latin, I'm sorry."

"Italian, and no need to apologize. It just means you need more fun," I roll on top of her and start gnawing on her neck, "with me," she giggles and snorts. I stop suddenly, lift my head and look at her. "What was that?" I ask smiling. She covers her face with the sheet.

"Oh my God, don't look at me."

"I find it hard not to," back at her neck.

"Stop, don't make fun of me," I kiss her nose and apologize. She goes back to lying on my chest, exhales and we both start laughing at her snort.

Ah... how I wish these lazy afternoons would never end; the problem with relaxation is that there comes a point when it becomes detrimental to ones' health. My gut tells me that time is coming in approximately 3...2...1... An abrupt pounding takes me out of my moment of reflection. Shit! That forty-five minutes I called safety time in the beginning is there for a reason; let's say a man works from 9 to 5, you know you just can't show up on the doorstep at 9 on the dot. He might have forgotten something and come back or slept late. This protocol saves me from such faux-pas' but has no power in the event that he comes home early.

"Michelle! Michelle! Who the fuck's in there?" still jingling the doorknob. "Open this Goddamn door. Michelle!" why would she? When someone's yelling at me, the last thing I want is to be in the same room as them.

"No one Max, I just showered," her face is the picture of panic, she's darting her head back and forth trying to think of something as he starts slamming his body against the door.

"Why the hell is the Goddamn door locked!" ooh, he sounds pissed. I really gotta go.

"I think I'll take my leave," I whisper. She jumps up trying to fix the room as best she can.

"What honey? The kids honey, don't want them walking in. Why are you home so early?" she yells to her beau as she picks up my shirt. I stand, take my button down and slide my arms through the sleeves. She helps fix my collar and kisses me, "alright, the window is open in the bathroom, just close the screen," I jumped out of the window, still attempting to button my shirt then I close the screen behind me. You're welcome Michelle Louis Parker, see you soon. XOXO.

Jumping out the window may seem a bit cliché, well that's because it is. The reason it's been done before is well it works, you know, dead men tell no tales. And may I say thank God for single story colonials, I once tried a fire escape exit… yeah… as cool as it sounds it doesn't work like in the movies, you get stuck about a story in the air. It looks a little suspicious when you're dangling off a ladder outside the window, and it makes you easy pickin's if he's carrying. The reason for my troubles you ask? Those ladder things are only meant for actual fires, so it takes like two people to pull it down all the way, three if it's really rusted. It's just not the best idea. So, as I was saying, I was stuck having to take a ten foot plummet onto garbage and dog shit, I wound up with part of a broken pencil embedded in my thigh smelling of excrement sprinting down an alley in the middle of Providence. This is my life. I'm sorry I haven't even introduced myself. Hi, my name is Jack Fabbrico, I think fast, act fast and as you can see I did learn something in my weekend as a boy scout. A.B.P. Always Be Prepared or in other words, cover your ass.

Now comes the difficult part, they will fight and bicker for a little while and she'll either give up on the fight and swear this was a one time thing and become more cautious or miraculously convince him that lil'Suzie Lee and James Dean were on the bus home, and she didn't want them walking in on her getting dressed, cus' come on. No matter how hot this mamma is, what kid wants to see that? That's what's tough for her, my end on the other hand, it will be a little more taxing. A text in the middle of the night on Monday or next Wednesday, the day before one of our appointments, it'll say something like *'Can we meet? We gotta talk,'* or something to that effect. She, the paranoid one, will suggest a diner or café, a real run down dive, just some shithole a town over. She'll want to be far away from her home and her hubby's workplace when she tells me that this can't happen anymore. So my choices are to stop or use my masters in bull shittery. I'll sniffle, gently grasp her hands and profess some deep feelings on how she is the light of my every waking moment maybe squeeze out a tear then as her heart is melting suggest we go to my place from now on for our little sexcapades so she may feel safer.

There is one huge flaw in all of that, not only will it intervene with my strict schedule and other relationships but it also could make this more serious than it needs to be and therefore more dangerous. I can't stop. It's not that I don't want to, which I don't, I just can't. It drives me. It kills the pain of boredom, hell I'd rather be shot in the gut and left in Death Valley than spend an hour in a room doing nothing. Sex, masturbation, flirting, the ritual, the art of the pursuit is what gets my blood pumping. Kissing that one girl you know you shouldn't will get your adrenaline up faster than any stimulant you may come across. That's what I'm about, discovering and living the most exciting and pleasurable life possible, but like all great thing in this world there are casualties. Regardless what I do I will be deemed the 'bad guy' by her and her husband and her friends. Well as my pappy said and his pappy before him: 'If it ain't broke too bad don't throw it away,' granted that's for cars, bikes and single engine planes but I feel it works here too. Come on, we all need a specialty.

I'm not dating that cheater in there, or dating at all in the conventional sense, this is not a romance story. This is just my life and my thoughts; put pen to paper and sharing it with, well, let's say a friend. She and I are hooking up. It's as plain as that. We met at the club, had a few drinks, talked philosophy, literature, and movies. She got a little loose, we danced a bit and I gave her my number in case she wanted to have more fun. The next day or the day after I received a text asking what I was up to and I replied with *'nothing'* she thanked me for the *'stimulating'* conversation. I asked if she wanted to get coffee, she was hesitant but after a few minutes of discussing the small things she circled back and agreed. I could imagine her sitting alone on her huge bed twisting her wedding band around her finger weighing the risks of seeing me and somehow convincing herself, 'it's just a cup of coffee.' As the story goes, as the story goes with all my inamoratas, one thing led to another and… I lost my head.

There was no great perusal just minor seduction. She knows the bare minimum about me which is best in all honesty. This is her affair, a purely sexual arrangement in which both parties agree not to risk the others safety or 'good' name. Though, it makes no difference to her husband. When guys' find out their gals aren't faithful they all turn into psychotic douches, it's a war of the worlds and there are bound to be casualties. Don't get me wrong I'm in no way shape or form a different breed, which is why I don't have a gal of my own. I am more evolved in one aspect, and that is my awareness of my faults. To compensate for this key character flaw I avoid real relationships, but I still am a man full of passion, so…I just borrow others. It's more fun that way.

He doesn't know who I am, Max that is, the guy back in the house there. Max wants to kill me, and he has every right, I won't deny that, he's entitled to wish I were dead. It's very healthy for him to want the worst of the worst to befall me; I mean who am I to him? I wonder what I look like in his head. I always think this whenever my playtime gets found out. There's nothing that can ease his mind, nothing I can do anyway, and even if she said it was a purely physical affair it still wouldn't settle his nerves. When someone cheats it's for one of two reasons: they are unhappy with their spouse or with their life in general. At the end of the day why they cheat is irrelevant: it look bad on their partner as not being enough to make them happy.

I aid the party at fault by trying to fulfill the physical desires that they, or more accurately their partner, might be lacking. But I take all precaution to avoid emotions. I keep my history a secret, rarely let them see where I live (there are a few exceptions as there are to all rules), I text opposed to calling, occasionally use an alias and never ask them the problems in their relationship: you have a bad day I'll listen, you hate a co-worker *she's a real bitch*, something cute your kid did *Aw...* but I don't want to know anything about your husband, boyfriend or girlfriend. It's fairly easy to be unknown in this day and age. People are so obsessed with talking about themselves that it could take months even years before they ask me my last name, and I laugh when everything is over. They might as well have just fucked a ghost.

I'm starting to get worried with this one though. The past couple weeks I've caught Michelle looking at my driver's license when I got out of the bathroom, asking me about my childhood and she's greeted me up the street a few times. I think she wants to know me as a person, make this more than it is, escalate. Know-me-know-me, you know. Yeah, you do. But she could also just want to talk; I mean what are you left with after the physical pleasure is over? You do need to talk and not be cold, be charismatic without appearing loving. Show affection but don't get too attached because at the drop of a hat everything could change and you need to be ready.

You see that's when it becomes unfair in my eyes, when she starts to feel for me then I have to scare her off by jumping the shark. She may feel guilty if I were to say something like 'I love you' and not want to hurt me as a friend, if you can call what we have a friendship. She'll keep seeing me for a little while but eventually she'll get less invested and emotionally detach herself, then she'll reduce texting, at some point just stop and we'll be through, and there will be no evidence that she ever knew me. But there is always the possibility that she does have strong feelings for me and the mortar of my tomb will be concrete. That's not good, the pun and the situation. Yes my time was cut short with her but only by a few minutes, today is Thursday my dear friend, my busiest day, and I can't spare a single iota. I gotta go.

**Thursday, 2:39pm, The Runaway**

In any group of guys, usually in their late teens to late twenties, there's always that one who says the age-old expression 'a whore is cheaper than a girlfriend/wife' or they make the argument that for the time and money one puts into a relationship they're not getting much in return for their investment. I guess they overlooked my profession. I'm not saying its' perfect; I'm essentially a commodity, I service them, I am theirs. I like to self-objectify. Like most things in life it's a give and take; less expensive than a hooker or a galpal, but you don't always get what you want. For me, it boils down to one incredibly important question. 'Would you rather your dick wet or your balls licked?' I rather be a plaything, I may not have a say in what happens during our sessions but at least I get immediate gratification, that's not always guaranteed in a relationship especially in the early stages of its development, and though you may get what you want the other way it'll cost you every time. I like what I do.

Recent statistics show that fifty-four percent of women admit to being unfaithful in any given relationship, that doesn't include those who lie. Fourteen percent of all married women have strayed at least once. And thirty-five, both men and women, have admitted to cheating while on business trips. Forty-one out of a hundred marriages, again both sexes, have had one or both parties cheating. Taking the fifty-four percent as our base and let's take the combined population of the three areas I frequent (New Bedford, Fall River, and Providence) which is about 362,000 people, half of which would be 181,000 women. Now we can plug in our 54 percent of cheaters, which gives me around 97,740 possible playmates. I know I'm not playing fair with these numbers, but I don't have the time to subtract minors, the elderly, and lesbians from my calculations.

I'm not what most people would consider a nice guy, but I'm not evil or malicious either, I'm just a cad. I seek out unavailable women; it's just my thing. It's fun; you're there only when you want to be and don't have to deal with the serious shit. I have fun with them; sex, games and yes I have at times played with their feelings. It's an ego thing. Any pseudo-psychologist, sociologist or graduate under women's or female studies, whatever the hell they call it these days, will accuse me of being insecure. They'll say I have low self-esteem, I fear commitment and other stupid shit. I don't deny their claims, they're absolutely right. However, the problem with asking those individuals about my situation is that they only look at half the problem, be it intentionally or unintentionally I don't know.

The source of my contempt you ask, well... I've been with one of these girls and heard it all. They will state that 'it's a problem that I'm solely at fault for' or a variation of that. It's their sense of sorority. The whispers are and always have been Jack is sleeping with this guy's wife, sleeping with that guy's girl. No one in all my days has ever said this guy's girl who supposedly loves him, unconditionally mind you, is cheating on him with some nobody named Jack. That's what gets my goat, they refuse to admit a good percentage of the blame should be put on the women who are willing to cheat, and it should. Just saying a person had a moment of weakness does not mean you are admitting that they are at fault; you're acknowledging them as something of pity not someone to be held accountable. I'm not exonerating myself, by no means am I a saint. I only want things to be seen as they truly are, wipe the doors of perception if I may quote Blake.

These mind fuckers use every trick to convince themselves and even try to convince me of some femi-bitch rationale that their cheating in some extent is empowering to them as women. My favorite explanation was when I was in college, as I've said I've been with a femi-bitch or feminazi, whichever term you prefer. Her name was Cat... why did I say 'was' I think she's still alive, sorry... anyway her name is Katy, but I called her Cat; she was cute, had a sweet smile, dark brown eyes, and long auburn hair. She had a little pudge around the belly but nothing that's too noticeable from the right angles, not that her looks mattered much to me anyway, I suppose it just made it easier for me to show her how beautiful she was in my eyes.

Cat was majoring in women's studies so sociology, human sexuality, gender law, history of great women blah-blah-blah. She explained her cheating to me as 'a form of self-liberation from the patriarchal structure of a heterosexual relationship.' That was something she actually said on multiple occasions. I would have laughed in her face if it wouldn't have hurt the terms of our relationship: she says something that she thinks sounds smart and uber-progressive and I applaud making her feel as though she's right. The problem I had with Cat and others like her is that it's all bullshit they're spouting. There's no great war that entitles them to break someone's heart for no fucking reason. And when caught they self-victimize as a way to alleviate themselves from the consequences. Avoiding responsibility is pretty much the most anti-feminist thing a woman striving for equality can do.

I know not all women like this, I am a stout equalist and some are honest in their cheating, but many have to rationalize it to themselves and honestly that's really a turn-off. I mean I'll prey on insecurities, daddy issues and or psychopathy but diarrhea of the mouth gives me extreme limp dick. Sorry, I got derailed and don't think that I'm bashing, I know or believe, that not all feminists are man-hating ego driven drones, but a good enough percentage are that some women who actually believe in equality of the genders fear to call themselves feminists so they won't be mistaken for these bitches. I've had to devise a test to see whether they're a true feminist or feminazi if you care to hear; if they think that the words suffrage and suffering are interchangeable you're looking down a Gestapo gal my friend. If they know it means the right to vote, then they're true and blue to the cause, to the latter I support thee.

Please don't mistake me for a misogynist just for my opinions, I love women especially those that can propose a good argument and I respect women who give respect in order to achieve it. I love a conversation in which the two parties may peacefully disagree, and at the end I won't be called an ignorant bastard just for voicing an opinion. With this said all I really want from a cheater is for her to say 'I'm a cheat, I stand by it. I'm not a bad person I'm just in need of some vitamin D now and again'. That's all I want. That's how you win my respect. I don't think it is too much to ask, do you?

Anywho, before I had to run off I was talking about why Michelle's feelings would be bad and how they would interfere with my schedule. I spend my time with her from 9:45am-

2:50pm then I have to go to my sisters' restaurant to help out with whatever she needs me to do which is usually balancing out the books. That takes about an hour, unpaid I'll have you know. Then I order my free meal because apparently, my assistance is worth at most fifteen bucks in non-transferable compensation. Then most likely I'll have to take Luke, my brother-in-law, outside for a whoopin' cus' I know he'll be screwing up my order for the umpteenth time. That may sound a bit rash for fucking up someone's food, but for the past three or four months, he's been doing this dumbass prank of saving my orders and making what I ordered the time before instead. It was funny the first couple of times when I had to think twice if I ordered that, but it got old fast, goes nowhere, and now it's just really pissing me off. I hit him upside the head every now and then and we go outside and duke it out, he thinks it's a game until I leave my mark but no matter how many times I knock him down he still does it, and I'm really gonna' give it to him today. Letting this pass would only encourage his idiotic pranks.

Where was I… right then, I must be off to my next dalliance which often happens around 4:45-5ish. Afterward, I head to the club, for work not play, I'm a bouncer from 9:30 pm to 2:30 am and help clean up which lasts until 3 am. Finally, I have an hour of TV then bed. It's a full schedule. If Michelle had me in anything that remotely resembled a real relationship, she would probably come to my sis' restaurant. There goes everything: being a jerk to my sister, beating up my brother-in-law and I don't think she would be keen on my fun with Siobhan, let alone the others in my Rolodex, I'd have to change my job. She may want me devoted to her and her alone, but there's no guarantee she'll return the favor, then what am I but a fool. Seriously can someone tell me when did organizing an elaborate ruse get so complicated? Anyone? Please…

I apologize if I'm coming off a bit brash. I am a man and what are we but the physical manifestation of what this world has taken from us. Those that come from (are damaged by) wealth tend to major in pomposity, those from high knowledge suffer from the inability to related to the common man, then what of those damaged by women, what is our flaw? Being mistaken for misogynists? The perpetual nursing of a broken heart? Being blind to actual emotion? Having a rager at all hours of the day? I don't know maybe you could help me find that out. Every man, no matter how confident, successful or righteous has a broken heart story. I do, now Maxi does, pretty sure you do too. So what does it mean? The pain of a broken heart. Does it mean we have lived? I sure hope so, because if not then these rhetorical questions would be kinda pointless. I'd tell you more, but I really have to get going before some ball busted ass gasket tries to kill me, laters.

**Thursday, 2:50pm, Forget About Domani**

My philosophy is all about living in the moment, why wait to do her tomorrow when she's wet now. It's always good to have a personal philosophy. I highly suggest having one of your own. And by that I mean make one up. Don't just pick mine or your best buds because it's right infront of you, that's no different than if you were to follow scripture, or a cult, or some crackpot conspiracy theorist preaching about aliens, it robs you of your own opinion. I mean the reason I ask so many questions is that I want to be disagreed with, opposition can ingrain an idea deeper, or it can enlighten one to the value of the opposing view. Hold on I gotta make a stop.

I pull into a minimart, that high pitched ding noise that gives warning to all of the two people within this thirty-five by fourty foot establishment rings. The clerk is a young girl, about nineteen or twenty. I have yet to meet a woman that a part of me hasn't fallen in love with for at least fifteen minutes. She looks quite sweet; her hazel eyes, a natural beauty mark that rests on her right cheekbone, dark hair with blonde highlights, even that red and black uniform drapes over her contours in a mildly sensual way. Her name, 'Beth', printed on the bit of plastic pinned on her breast. She's either engaged or engaged to be engaged by her high school sweetheart; his class ring is on a golden chain with a heart shaped locket at its side, he was born in July.

"A pack of Marlboros," I say as I look down pulling out my wallet.

"Those thing's a' kill ya," her smile is beaming.

"Is life worth living if you have to abstain from everything?"

"Deep, but I think people should stay away from things that are known to be deadly. Anything else?" am I really getting a lecture from a gas station attendee?

"Maybe I wanna die, a rose please. Red."

"Aww, don't say that," why are you so concerned? "That comes to 14.95."

"Here," I hand her fifteen.

"Thank you," I plop the nickel in the take a penny tray.

"You're young, wait five years, and you'll see more people will agree with me than you."

"Huh?" you're lucky you're cute.

"In the immortal words of Woody Allen, 'I could live to be a hundred if I gave up everything that would make life worth living' or something like that."

"Smart man, who's Woody Allen?" mental face palm, what a world we live in.

"Nobody, just some guy who married his daughter."

"Ew, no way," she pulls out her phone, I can see her typing his name on the screen she misspelled Woody with 'Wudie.'

"She isn't biologically related to him. God, go see a movie now and again," I'm at most seven years older than her, can there really be this big of a gap in taste? She has to be an outlier on the bell curve. People just aren't like this in reality, are they?

"Ok…"

"Trust me; you'll like him," I pick up the cigarettes and flower, smack the head of the pack in the palm of my hand then leave.

What is beauty without brains? Youth is a double-edged sword; the firm tightness of their bodies doesn't make up for the vast gabs in their knowledge. I would, if I didn't just screw up in there by losing my cool, have tried to make a move. I'd ask her opinions on random bullshit and pretend to care. I'd tell her she's so bright, make her feel special. Once you do that, once you get in their heads you get in their hearts, then you get in their beds.

See that ten year old sky blue sedan parked by the dumpster, just out of sight from the minimarts windows, that's a first-time car. The pail sweet color indicates that the owner is most likely female. For the past year, it's been parked in that same spot every time I've come here and she cashed me out. Deduction my dear Watson. Time to make an apology; I walk over to the car, lift the wiper and pinch the rose underneath. I'll make my apologies in person next-time I come around.

She's too young for me and I know it, but you can't blame a guy for trying. It's not that I'm old, I say she's too young because I tend to go after women more age appropriate.

Actually, the majority of those I keep in frequent contact with are at least two or three years older than me. There's a point they hit in life where they begin to question every relationship they have: friends, family, co-workers, you name it, they will at one time or another ask themselves 'does this person make me happy?', I like them like that. They either know exactly what they want, or they don't and it becomes an adventure. This time in their lives, their late twenties to early thirties, is usually when they begin to accept that they settled for the first guy that sounded like a good deal and it's been about five-six years of being a good hausfrau. Now it's time to be a little naughty. They're still in contact with their college (or even high school) friends, so why not have a girls' night out once in a while? Go to the club, the movies, maybe a bar, they just need to live a little and that's when they meet guys like me. I am a wolf stalking sheep. I take note of everyone in the group.

I drift into the outer circuit and watch. I see them, all of them: the pretty, the angry, the soulful, the hopeful and the disturbed. I take my notes, sizing up my prey. I'm going for the disturbed, I usually go for the disturbed. She's the one who's insecure. Who always feels alone. Who always feels as though she's doing something wrong. Presumed guilt will draw one into doing something they'll regret pretty quickly, that's just the way they see themselves. They all want to be a bad girl at heart.

Almost every pack consists of the same three to five women. One or two of them are happily married the others are in long term relationships, or single and proud of it, and then there are the special ones. The ones who need to escape their homes, their living graves. I look at the ones that appear to always have something to say but remain silent, they're alone even around friends. I can help her. I know I can. She goes to the bar or concession stand or bathroom, there's my chance. I drift in and out of the crowds, I'm close but she doesn't see me, I turn to my side, take a step backwards and bump into her. I apologize then say 'hello' they return the favor blaming themselves for my accident. I comment on their clothes or hair and they thank me, thus begins our conversation. Just a conversation to start; a conversation where she is the only subject, where I want to know everything about her, where for one moment in a very long time she feels appreciated, even adored. That is the moment where she forgets about tomorrow, but this is the moment where I have to abstain. Always leave them wanting more.

**Thursday, 3:05pm, Detained**

Heading to Anne's Diner, the day is beautiful. Only a few clouds, low seventies or low twenties if we're going metric. These are the days I wish I was insecure enough to have bought convertible, but I can still enjoy the weather with the windows down. I love that feeling of the wind fluttering over my shirt, the air whipping through each gap between my buttons. Peace comes and peace goes. I hear the sirens, cop not Greek, instead of pulling over right away I guess I'll drive an extra hundred yards or so. Sorry officer... I pull to the shoulder looking down the long road ahead. My hands locked on the wheel, the breeze stills and the heat pours in this black metal box. I lean my elbow out the window, run my fingers through my hair and look at the passenger seat as a ladybug flies in. It takes a rest on the hot leather. Slowly crawling up the backrest; following the seam as best she can. Halfway up, the bug stops at a node and flips its wings but doesn't fly away, it just rests. Suddenly I hear the skid of shoes grinding sand into the pavement, a shadow approaches. The swine clears its throat. I close my eyes, inhale and open them, still facing the passenger's seat. My little love has flown away.

"Do you know why I pulled you over," it's a woman's voice, sweet and cold. I'm going to be so fucking late. Anne is going to ream me. I move my hand over to get my registration from the glove compartment. "Sir, look at me when I am talking. Do you know why I pulled you over?"

"No... Rachel?" I finally saw who it was under all that authority. She looked the same since I saw her last: hadn't gained weight, hadn't gotten wrinkles or yellow teeth, so little to no cigarette contact. She is still remarkably fair. A thin lock of her red hair curled on her forehead from under her cap, her eyes covered by cheap sunglasses.

"How ya been?" she has the biggest grin on her face and still with that tone of authority, she speaks informally letting her punky roots show.

"I'm good, Raunch... shit sorry, Rachel... officer. I'm so screwed," she starts to laugh.

Rachel Almeida, or Raunchy as she came to be known by the fine people in Roosevelt, was an old friend I hadn't seen in about nine or ten years. I knew her at the start of middle school maybe the end of elementary. She's famous in these parts for getting caught giving head to Mr. Souza, our gym teacher, in seventh grade for an 'A,' hence her nickname Raunchy, or the Rauch. Souza got arrested, and she played the story in her favor, using the victim status in class for an easy ride and the harlot reputation as cred. People snickered behind her back whenever she bragged about her expertise in the boudoir, everyone knew she was lying. No one would be with a chick that got the last guy she sucked arrested. A beautiful girl with an easy ride and guys too afraid to talk to her, obviously she was hated by every girl in school. I say, or at least believe, she only had two real friends which consisted of my sister Anne and myself. We three were family; except for when I had a date, then I guess I left them to their own social devices. But once Anne started dating seriously, Rachel was all alone. I promised her that regardless if I had a gal pal or not I would always be there, and I kept it as best I could.

I looked after her throughout high school, you could say I wrote the book on modern chivalry. I was almost expelled once for choking a kid out when I heard the word 'slut' scape his lips. I was ruthless, especially to this girl Sara who spread a rumor that my Rachel was preggers, I got in one beautiful act of vengence. Some would say I snapped. I got a hold of a naked picture of this chick, don't ask me how, and I had a friend who was really into visual editing help me photoshop a dick on her (he really made it look natural). Then we sent it from a ghost account to half the school with a caption that read *TRANNY ALERT*. I don't know if after that she transferred or what, all I knew is that Rachel was avenged. I was her mad dog ready to pounce, ready to protect my mistress. Rachel was my closest friend and I wouldn't abandon her, I would do anything for her.

Halfway through our senior year she disappeared, no word about it. I was worried. Her cell didn't work so I called her house to get a disconnected drone, no replies to my emails, so I eventually walked three miles to her place to see nothing. No car in the driveway, her basketball hoop was gone, her house was empty with a sign that read *East Coast Realty* in her front lawn. I dedicated my teen years to her, and I don't even get a goodbye. Did I mean anything to her? After ten days of me locking myself away and tearing apart my room in random fits of rage I received a letter, the return address was somewhere in North Carolina. The letter consisted of a two-page apology and her new cell number. We kept in touch for a couple of months but texted less and less as we got into our first semester and eventually lost contact altogether, as kids inevitably do. I never imagined her as a defender of the law, putting men in jail yes but a copper? No. So I was a bit frozen when I realized Raunchy was a piglet.

"What? Surprised I'm back or that I'm a cop now Johnny Boy?" a bit of both.

"We've been over this a hundred times so let me be frank I go by Jack," I fall back into our highschool rutine.

"So are you Frank or Jack?" she giggles.

"Stupid when we were kids, stupid now," pulling out her pad, her smile drops, and the stern feeling returns. I hate this.

"Are you belittling the authority of an officer of the law? That can be and may be construed as verbal assault," she taps the tip of the pen against her tongue.

"Are you serious?" she breaks character and laughs.

"Wow, no fight? That's not the Jack I remember, the old or may I say *young* Jack would've argued, he would've said I was abusing my power or prattled off the definition of 'verbal assault' ya somehow memorized in an attempt to make me feel dumb or something. Getting dull are we?"

"Raunchy… Why are you doing this to me? I wasn't speeding, and I only killed two pedestrians back there."

"Your blinker's been on the past couple miles."

"What? Is that a ticket-able offence?"

"It is a *fineable* offence, yes, but I will let you go with a warning under two conditions, you A. turn your blinker off now and B. we catch up. I moved back, and've been in the area for a while, but finally, finally! I'm settled. And after all this time I still don't know anyone."

"Are you propositioning me Raunchy?" wait, what do you mean been here a while?

"That's Officer Raunchy and no, I uh… got married," she stammered target acquired.

"No, kiddin' you got hitched."

"Yep, so… can we catch up?"

"Well if my only other option is being ticketed then I guess I have no choice. Sure, sounds fun, I'm not doing anything tomorrow. So… dinner at my place?"

"No dinner, Max wouldn't like that," Max? Really?

"And Max is your… husband?"

"Yes… any problems with that."

"No, no it's just a surprisingly common name."

"How can something be both surprising and common?"

"Life finds a way Rachel. Life finds a way of making impossible things possible. So no dinner, how about lunch; no wine, dance or romance just a bland lunch, would that make Maxi feel comfortable."

"Lunch will be fine…" she laughs. "Here's my number," she writes her cell number on the back of a card she pulled from her pocket and gives it to me.

"That's strange."

"What?"

"You just said you were married, but your card reads Officer Rachel T Almeida. J'you lie to me?"

"There's that eagle eye," she smiles and walks away. I punch the number into my phone and send *Fabbrico*, I watch her through my side mirror. She stops on her way back to the cruiser, pulls out her phone and looks back. I think I see a smile. The game is on. Also just wondering, why do officers have cards anyway? Don't they all have the same number? I drove off as she entered her car.

**Thursday, 3:23pm, Jack the Dull Boy**

I enter the diner from the back; I park in front of the dumpster, right between the restaurant and an old grocers stand. The stench of old fryer grease and sun-baked garbage fills the air, it smells a little like bad parmesan nesting in spoiled milk. The scent of salt and cream, and dirt, and grass; it's strange how some things can be both repulsive and pleasant. Entering through the kitchen; hoping to avoid conflict, no big deal, just going to sneak into the office. Fuck! Of course now is when Anne has to be chopping onions for salads. Crap! She planned this, she fucking planned this.

My big sis is not only the owner of this establishment but a waitress, grill cook, prep person and general overseer of product. She looks pretty pissed. Not even the onions can get a tear from her.

"Late," she mumbles.

"What?"

"You're late, again."

"You don't even pay me," she slams the knife on the counter.

"What's the point in helping if you can't even show up on time?" she won't look me in the eye.

"God damn Anne, I put pencil to paper I think it can wait ten minutes now and again, are the books in the office?"

"Yes, and lower your voice."

I was about to walk down the stairs when the ice machine clicked on, I turned around and looked back at Anne. Still focused on those onions.

"Hey uhhh... do you remember Rachel?"

"Who?"

"Raunchy, remember Rachel from school?"

"I 'member," she finally looks me in the eye, she smiles for a second then opens her mouth slightly. Her eyes look to the side, then up, and her tongue wipes the back of her upper left canine, she closes her mouth looking back at me with the same smile, "I remember *Raunchy Rachel blew coach Souza, she'd do anything to increase her grade, she said she couldn't fail but now he's in jail, and he thought he was gettin' laid,*" she snickers. I always hated that limerick; don't know why I made it.

Oh yeah…that's right. I wanted to keep other guys from planting their flags in my mountain. Nothing kills a boner like the possibility of unwanted sodomy in the communal shower at county. Yes, I was friend-zoned, badly, and I'm still a bit raw about it.

"Yeah, and why do you still have that memorized? That was like fourteen years ago."

"I have my reasons, what about her?"

"She pulled me over. I mean she's a cop now and pulled me over."

"A cop? No, not the Raunch."

"Yeah, married too. Anyway, I gotta hit the books," walking down to the office I can hear her chuckling, laughing even.

Most small businesses fail immediately. I know this, Anne knows this, but she still poured a shit load of money into a small diner on the northern recesses of the Dartmouth border. I, out of idiocy or generosity which many times are the same thing, offered my assistance. When I made that offer I thought she would ask me to put up some drywall, install an outlet, fix the boiler or something, you know, manual labor. Not talking me into balancing her finances. I took one accounting class, one. I didn't even do that good; I think my best grade I got was an eighty-five.

What I do is simple, I try to see what can be done to lower her expenses; food, drink, silverware, dishes, how cheap she can get them and how much she can flip 'em. Finally, she got into the black after six years of scrimping, working hundred hour weeks and training employee after employee, paying off all her debts and alienating every last one of her friends and relatives. I guess she still can't pay me. Women are crazy that way.

My sister is the last bit of family I have, dad left when I was nine she was twelve, and our mom passed away a few years ago. I really should stop complaining about her. Anne is just a little too complicated for my liking; I love her to death but she infuriates me more often than not. Being the elder sibling, of course, I was her toy from birth until dad left, that whole Oedipal complex thing gets really confusing when you're being forced in a dress, or when you have two prominent female figures in your life that are so different in personality. Maybe that's why I can't be with one girl. Our mom was a tad off. As kids we loved how much fun she was, I cherish almost every memory I have of her. She was silly and playful. She was like a kid when dealing with us. But when you're a child you don't notice the difference between kooky and crazy.

Rationalizing things we don't understand is something people do, and that's what we did with mom. She would occasionally speak to herself, anyone's first thought would be something normal like 'she's just thinking out loud,' right? Then she would go a day or two without bathing: she is going green, water conservation. These are the logical conclusions Anne came up with and told me, I can't remember what I thought about her actions. When she was fun she was fun when she wasn't I don't know, I probably thought she was possessed or something. There are some gaps in my memory when I was a babe and Anne tells me they're things I don't want to know. With these matters I tend to trust her judgement.

I was thirteen when I realized that mom had a few screws loose. The first real sign something was wrong that I noticed had to have been her mood swings. I would see her laughing one minute then the next she would be silent staring out the window, and a look of melancholy would show throughout her composure, almost as if someone tampered with the room's lighting and shone blue on her face. If something was the slightest out of place she would either cry or start throwing things screaming. The memory of her running at me with my sneaker in hand raised above her head, yelling, eyes bursting out as black holes in a red ocean is forever burned in my mind as one of the most terrifying experiences of my life. She looked like a flying daemon coming after my soul.

By my fourteenth birthday her motor skills had declined severely, so much so that we feared to go within arms-reach; she would tremble and flail, abrupt violent outbursts became normal for her or who she had left us with. By the time I was sixteen, Anne had taken over all motherly duties, she took care of mom for a few months until it became impossible and we had no choice but to have her institutionalized. As soon as we saw the first doctor he pulled her records and filled Anne in on what was happening.

Marla San Fabbrico, a year before dad left, had lost control of the old sedan and drove into a light post suffering minor injuries. Upon examination, the attending physician noticed a persistent tremor in her hands, yet her heart rate stayed relatively normal, with no other signs of traumatic stress she was asked to stay for observation. Blood tests, MRI's, all came back negative. She was then sent to a neurologist for examination. Be it a hunch or she wanted to rack up the bill a genetic test was ordered. The results showed an abnormality. There was a mutation in the trinucleotide repeat of her HTT gene, normal is between ten and thirty-five repeated sequences of the CAG codon, she had fifty-three. This particular mutation is cause for the production of protein mHTT accelerating neural atrophy in the cerebral cortex and basal ganglia. Huntingtin's. She never told us, and suddenly everything made sense.

Mom was hospitalized two times before she was committed; the second of which she attacked Dan, our father, with a lamp accusing him of cheating. The proof that she had was a phone number in his wallet. The number was of a woman, yes, but she was mom's neurologist. Understandably, he left but kept in contact with her doctor, our 'aunt' Sadie who would stay for a few days a month. I was unaware that any of this was happening around me.

Anne kept this hidden from me for a while; she's the one who called Sadie when mom went off her meds. I assume Anne believed that she was protecting me. It wasn't until she was in her early twenties and decided to have us both tested that she felt it necessary to tell me. Anne is clear, I opted out of seeing my results, but allowed her to see them.

Our father knew everything and helped out whenever he could, from a distance. When he left, Anne began receiving letters and checks from him every couple of days, and she would reply. In the early stages of her diagnosis, when mom went to therapy or work he'd drop by to check in, work on her car and even make repairs to the house. His visits stopped when I was about eleven or twelve. I remember I got a phone call from him a few days after I turned thirteen.

"How you doin', son?"

"Ok, I guess. Mom broke my Batmobile."

"How?"

"She threw it, the right wing snapped off."

"Does it still drive?"

"Yes."

"You know what I always say."

"If it ain't..."

"Shhhhh... good boy. You can probably just glue it on, right?"

"I guess. When can I see you?"

"How's your sister?"

"Fine, when can I see you?"

He's silent.

"Dad..."

"Can I talk to your sister?"

"Fine," I handed Anne the phone, and she walked into the next room. When she came back she told me dad is busy with work and he feels that if mom were to see him they would just get into another fight and he doesn't want us to see that.

A few months later, I felt I was just getting the runaround from him and stopped answering the phone. He sent me a letter, I burned it in the yard. Anne beat the shit out of me that day, but I didn't care, I didn't want anything to do with him anymore. Anne was his favorite anyway. He helped pay for this diner and she still occasionally gets lunch with him. The last bit of contact I had was when I graduated from Dartmouth. Anne invited him to my walking ceremony, from the stand I could see him in the crowd smiling, cheering and pointing at me saying, 'that's my boy,' and 'I'm so proud,' but once the hats flew and we three had a little family reunion he put his hand out for me to shake, I took it and he said to me, 'You did more with that brain than I could've,' I don't know what that meant. I don't want to know. To me it was such a backhanded compliment that I knew I was right to cut him out. He walked away almost immediately after I shook his hand. The second he was out of earshot, I looked to Anne and said, 'Nothing, I want nothing from him. No letters, no checks, no contact,' I know he was trying to be kind, but that doesn't really change anything now, does it?

I learned to cope with isolation. If there's one thing I've learned, it's that familial bonds are as fragile as any other relationship. You add the slightest bit of stress and the entire structure collapses in on itself, I mean how many marriages are shattered by a child's death. I get it, death do you part and nobody said who had to die. The idea of family is flawed because it depends on strength and people by nature are weak; we lie, we cheat, we mislead. The honest truth is that when you wipe away the fairytales and superhero's we break far too easy. Emotionally Anne was devastated and we could never reconnect. The paradigm had shifted, she was suddenly an authority figure with dominion over me. Not just an older sister but a parent as well, Anne was forced to became an adult when she was sixteen, of course we don't see eye to eye. She never got over the loss of mom's mind. I guess I never got over the loss of my sister's heart.

She has since come out of her shell upon meeting Luke, I mean he's a total tool, and she could do way better but there is just something about him that can get her to smile, and when I look into her eyes as she laughs I believe it's sincere. He's a high school dropout, well off family, but he personally is not rich. Luke is pale for someone whose parents are off the boat from Portugal. At heart he's a good guy but lets his temper and dumb jokes get the better of him far too often. When he moved in with Anne, though I protested I have to admit a huge financial burden was lifted almost immediately. No matter how much he helped out, I just can't get over his dumb jokes; egg on a cracked door, putting my hand in warm water while I slept, it was like living with a child. No matter how happy he makes my sister I'm always going to hate his sense of humor.

I finished looking over her sales. Her profits have increased by nine percent since I checked last, so now it's time for my meal. Last week I ordered a Portuguese Burger, but I was given fish n' chips, today is steak and potatoes. If I get the fucking burger I am literally going to slap Luke in the face with the plate. Waiting… waiting… ten minutes and my steak comes out medium rare. He did it right? He did it right! And the green taste of disappointment comes up in my throat. You know when you expect something, whether-it-be good or bad, and it doesn't

38

happen you feel empty. I was looking forward to smacking him around. Not that I carry some deep seeded hatred or have any personal qualm with him other than he being the occasional asshole, I just already had it in mind to hit him. I don't know, I'm weird like that.

"Hey Luke! Luke!"

"Yeah John."

"Damn it, it's Jack."

"What do you want?" he came out still with a bruise on his cheek from the last time I gave him the back of my hand.

"What about your joke?"

"Joke?" don't play dumb you fucker.

"Your joke! You giving me the wrong food over and over again."

"Got tired."

"Oh, you got tired," or... learned your lesson?

Tired? Do you believe this shit, he was keeping this joke up for months, months... plural, if he did it two or three times fine, or if he built up to something like burying me in every order I made, that would have been entertaining. But nothing at all? Are you as pissed as I am? I guess he finally got the punch line; sorry, I wasn't trying to be punny again. And as I'm freaking out in here I probably, though I'm holding a lot back, look very frustrated which is why he's starting to laugh.

"You can go back now, just go."

"You sure?" he's still smirking.

"Yeah."

"Kay."

"Piss off."

Simplicity: was his joke just to wind me up and watch me go? Shit for brains.

"Hey, John," he's still an ass, "Anne wanted me to give you this," it's a piece of paper, if this is a bill so help me God. It's not a bill for the food or a check for all my hard work but a note, it reads:

*Jack I love you and I know you don't want to hear it but I still have to look after you. I can't see you like that again. For*

39

*your own good, stay away from Rachel. Please listen to me for*
*once.*
        *-Anne*

Fuck her, dare I respond on the other side of the paper? I dare:

*Dear Anne*
        *I appreciate your concern for my emotional well-being,*
*but in case you haven't noticed, I am not the little boy I once*
*was. I don't know what happened between you two and frankly, I*
*don't care. You are the only family I have, and I love you, though*
*I may not always show it, case in point my feuding with that ass*
*munch of a husband you got. But I let you live your life, so stop*
*thinking you have the right to intervene in my sex, or hope to be,*
*sex life. Thank you and good bye.*
        *-your lil' bro-bro*

I finished my food and was so angry that I stole the tip the guy
sitting next to me left, then got the H.E. double hockey sticks out
of there before I went on a rant yelling and give them both the
satisfaction of seeing me so distraught. Now I'm aiming to go to
Pleasant Street to pay a visit to Misses Dylan. And yes it is very
pleasant, I too love irony.

**Siobhan Dylan, Thursday 5:14pm, Mistake: Strike One**
    Siobhan the shrink... I like Siobhan: she's smart, charismatic, admits that she's really horny and calls me out on all my B.S., which I have to respect. The drive to her is a tad far if I'm coming from the diner, but on such a beautiful day why would I care. There is however a slight problem with her place; it's relatively close to my personal abode so there is always the chance I may have a run in with her and hubby at the store or something, *c'est la vie* I suppose. I park at the minimart just before her house, sneak through the back, hop over the fence and look there she is; her arms crossed, a cigarette betwixt the good doctor's fingers, sitting on the patio lounge, catchin' some rays. She's letting her hair down, she knows what I like. We're not even discrete anymore, her sitting poolside and me jumping over a fence for all the neighborhood to see. Stupid I know but I do this because it makes her smile, and without that smile I'd be nothing. She's wearing a brown spandex onesie today which I find odd: one, she has the body for a two piece and two, she has much better taste than to have picked out that atrocious garment.
    "Sorry there Joan, for my uh... lateness," she doesn't mover her head or take off her sunglasses.
    "I'm sticking my neck out and you're late," she looks agrivated.
    "Joani, you're home alone. It's not like your husband down the hall, and we're getting it on in the closet," she giggles and pushes up her glasses, ah memories.

    I was once employed by her husbands' boss Muriel, she was having an event for her firm and needed a party bartender who was refined, could be polite and attentive but didn't want to spend catering prices so through a text by my Joani I placed a few fliers around the area and sent an email or two and I was called up a few days before the event. This was the first time I met Joani's husband, I never caught his name; he's kind of an oaf, a hard worker but blind to the world around him, the basic definition of a cog.
    He is the type of guy who orders a Manhattan, hates the taste but still drinks it because that's what his superiors drink. At some point in the evening he asked me to add simple syrup or

something to make it tolerable. I looked at him then at his boss and said, "look she can handle it, be a God damn man and drink it," after that he took deeper swigs, after finishing his first glass the second went down easier. Just a side note I think he's fucking Muriel now; he's out later and shows up to work earlier, this is what Siobhan tells me. She doesn't think he is or maybe she's just in denial, either way our little meetings can be more fluid.

Any-whosies, I took a half hour break when everyone was good and liquored up, I noticed Mister Dylan was talking informally with his boss. Siobhan was openly flirting with me in front of her husband, she was talking about when we first met and how boring the party is, the good sir didn't even notice. We took a walk to the master bedroom, went in the walk-in-closet and had a little fun. I pinched it and blew a load in someone's coat pocket.

"I know, but I also know what kept you. I don't like having to share Jacky-boy."

"Well look at it from my perspective, I gotta share you. He gets you for a while, she gets me for a while. It all works out in the end."

"I share you with one other man, one!" her voice raises, she slams her leg against the chair and takes a pause, "I know you got more than one girl. A little black book even," a Rolodex actually but thanks for playing, "it's not fair Jack and don't try to bullshit me."

"Fair? What's fair? Is this fair to him? Or me?"

"Things don't have to be fair for you. You're not like a... real person, you don't have to follow their rules."

"Reality is far too potent a drug for me. That's why I tend to take my doses few and far between."

"Cute."

"Well I try."

"See... that's what I love about you," she pauses looking at me with a vacant expression, clears her throat and stammers, "l-like about you. That's why we're friends. Norms are so fucking boring. I don't want someone who gets and gives what's deserved, I want someone who shrugs off the serious stuff and has some fun," she put her glasses back on and folds her hands over her stomach.

"Wait a minute-wait a minute, you just backtracked a shit ton right there."

"How so?"

"You just said things aren't fair. Implying that it's a bad thing then continued by saying you like that I don't play fair. That sounds pretty contradictory to me."

"Not at all, I *like* that you stack the deck in your favor, it makes you more interesting. But sometimes I feel jipped. All I ask is you toss me a hand now and again."

"So you want me to give up everyone else and just be your side guy? Sorry but..."

"I never said that. Live your life as you want I just want you to be fair to me, be here when you say you'll be here or maybe I won't pick up next time you call."

"Kay... so can we go inside?" it feels like it just dropped twenty degrees.

"We probably should," she sucks halfway down her cigarette and doesn't move.

"Shall we vamoose?"

"Yeah," still she sits.

"How do I know I'm the only one?"

"Because I say so," *and I believe whatever she says.* Ok I do, but she has always been upfront with me. Prolonged silence. It's a little awkward now, I know she wants me to beg but can I really give in so soon?

"So... what time should I leave?"

"Whenever you want, now if you're not up to snuff," she sniffs and put the cigarette out on the ground.
I have to give it to her, even if it's sardonic.

"Please, oh please, may we go inside. I have missed you so."

"There we go," she smirks, spreads her legs, sits up and straddles the chair, "lose the tude next time," she turns to one side and stands. "So what's on the menu tonight?" wouldn't you like to know? I put my arm around Doctor Strangeloves waiste, and she walks me inside.

We went in through the sliding glass doors. Ever since I met Siobhan, Joani, I have, and still do, get dumbstruck by the inside of her house. The outside is very modest: eggshell vinyl siding, no garage, no floral decoration to greet company and a small front yard. The only appearance of luxury is the pool, patio and mechanized awning all of which are very common in this neighborhood. One might come to the conclusion that the plainness of this home is what makes it stand out, the surrounding homes are larger, have garages, their vinyl is more expressive: white, yellow, blue or beige. Some have pillars at the door, their drive and walk ways show wealth just by always appearing new, you can tell they get paved at the first sign of wear. The topiaries are always neat and presentable, the front yards potted flowers are changed seasonally. Nay, what makes this house stand out, other than the gorgeous creature that dwells within, is the interior. It's shimmering in wealth like a misers' wet dream.

The living room: sunk down half a step with hardwood floors, a 75" tv resting over the gas powered fireplace framed in granite, the walls are painted in a black, grey and white striped pattern, the etched flower and leaves design on the baseboards have a near silver tinge to them. There's an impractical but nice looking white carpet under her furniture, black post-modern couch and chairs that surround a glass table facing the tv. The style is new age with a hint of classical elegance. It looks as though it would be on the cover of some furniture mag.

There's only one picture in this place, it rests on the end table in the far off corner of the room specifically out of sight from most guests. It's a framed ultrasound. Angelique her name would have been. I think she'd be about three by now if it weren't for the heroin-infused maniac that sideswiped Joan's car at ninety miles an hour causing her to miscarry. I imagine that was the turning point in her life; the exact moment when she gave up the idea of a happy family and began to drift. Tumbling into a ditch, hanging upsidedown by your seatbelt, steeringwheel smashing into your chest and baby bump, head angled onto the roof with shards of windshield two inches from your eyes while your inner thighs are being coated in layer upon layer of blood, placenta and fetal matter gushing from your genitals, the cold empty feeling that life, a new life, has quite literally fleed your body tends to make you question everything. If a God could allow that, then I wonder what I could get away with. About a year later she met me, I like to think I made her see that it wasn't her fault, there was nothing that could've been done, especially by her. Even if I did it doesn't matter, I was too late. She's already like me, damaged.

Enough backstory, we walk, well chase each other through her stainless steel kitchen to the upstairs bedroom, our bedroom. Is it, or can it be a betrayal of the marital bed if we have sex in the guest room? She's still in her bathing suit. I can't wait for that thing to drop, not just to screw, I really hate that shit colored suit. I pull her in close, she wraps her arms around my neck. Kissing my Joani is like sticking my tongue in an outlet; pure energy titillating my lips and my tongue, my heart feels as though it's about to stop. We have lift off. I shut the door, and she removes her bathing suit. I walk up to my Joani and push her on the bed. Her legs spread; I unbutton my shirt and dive in face first.

An hour and a half, a sore jaw and several back scratches later we were coated in each other's sweat. We are laxed, exhausted and strung out on spunk, just letting those sweet neurotransmitters do their thing. Looking at the ceiling fan, I couldn't help but think of this afternoon. She starts with the psychoanalysis, what else about my childhood? I like to keep things a secret so I've just been making things up every time she tries analyzing me, she thinks it's fun.

"Well when I was thirteen I killed my neighbors' cat."

"Oh no," she jokingly responds.

"Yeah, and then I got a real taste for it. I killed the neighbor boy too; jammed a cactus up his ass and crucified him upside down on their front door," speaking as seriously as possible.

"How'd they take that?"

"Son of a bitch, the funny thing is they didn't notice."

"Not very attentive, I would say."

"Don't get me started. Once a week I would break in their house dressed like a clown," she's laughing so hard she's trying to stifle herself, "walk into their room and say I was their dead son."

"And what would they say?"

"'Which one?'"

"Either one."

"No that's what they said 'which one?'" she stops laughing and looks more serious.

"Is that how you see yourself? A clown?"

"Stop tryin' to figure me out," I put my right hand behind my head.

"Come on, I would love to take a peek into that mind of yours."

"Nah."

"How about just a brain scan then?"

"No tests."

"Afraid of hospitals, are we?"

"I'm not, I don't know about you, can't we just drop it?"

"Ok," and we lay in silence.

I close my eyes and try to relax again. What do I know of Siobhan and what does she know about me? I know that she and her husband met in college and a few months after graduation got married, they both attended Amherst. They waited until she got her doctorate to try for kids. Her accident caused a blood clot to form around her ovaries. The clot got infected scarring the area and leaving her infertile. She is a psychiatrist by trade, clinical. She's allergic to penicillin and pollen and looks particularly cute when spring hits, and she sneezes and twitches her nose every few seconds. Her favorite movie is Roberto Benigni's *Life is Beautiful.* When she was a girl, her favorite color was blue and now it's orange. What she knows about me: where I work, where I was born and where I'm ticklish. I've been with her for a while, usually, an affair lasts six months to a year somehow we've made it to two with no signs of stopping. I think today is our anniversary. I grab her hand interlock fingers and hold it above my heart.

"Hey Siobhan do…"

"Why do you do that?" she turns her head to me, wide eyed.

"Do what?"

"You call me Joan when I'm mad but Siobhan when I'm calm, why?" I crawl on top of her and kiss her nose.

"Cus' me thinks Joani sounds better than Siobhani when I'm trying to be sweet, anyway back to my question, wanna drink?"

"Sure, I think I have a little vodka in the freezer."

"I meant at a bar," her face drops.

"What! No, rule one idiot. Rule one!"

She is referring to THE FIVE RULES of cheating.

- Rule one. Never go out together, it's obvious.
- Numero Dos. Always wear a rubber. Do I really need to explain?
- Three. Do not get emotionally attached. It is awful, never do it, once a cheat always a cheat.
- Four. Always know points of egress. Great for running away. This rule can also be seen as always have a plan, I don't know, I just like the word egress.
- Five. If the guy ever confronts you, never make a promise. If you break it, you're going to disappoint him as well.

"I know," I start nibbling her ear, "I just want to do something," she pushes me away.

"You want to do something, go do it. Fuck what if my husband sees?"

"What would he be doing at a bar right now?" I go after her neck, she rolls off the bed and I'm left with a mouth full of pillow.

"Not the point. Are you falling for me? You want more now, is that it?"

"What! No, no. I just thought we're friends, your words, and we could grab a drink now and again."

"That is called a date if you're sleeping with the person," how narrow is your definition?

"Can you hand me my pants?"

"What?"

"In the chair behind you, I need my phone," she throws them at me.

"Why?" I pull out my phone.

"I need to text myself."

"Why?"

"I left my diary in the car, keep talking I just need to send a few key words," I type *Joan, fight, rules, text, DISCUSSION ON WHAT IT MEANS TO BE A FRIEND.*

"Why do you keep a diary?"

"Cus' I have nothing to say and a lot of words to say it in. Now back to the initial argument, you must recall that we met over drinks, at a bar, we talked for hours in front of people. So I'm confused. What's the big deal?"

"I'm married," she flails her arms.

"Yeah and look where it's gotten you?"

"You asshole! Please leave."

"Ok, ok. I just wanted to hang out didn't mean to ruin your day."

"Leave, go 'hang out' then."

"What's the matter with you, am I just a fucking toy?"

"No."

"Then what? Explain so I can better understand our situation. What exactly am I to you?"

"A... I guess... I don't know. Definitely not my boyfriend."

"Ok great, I don't want to be your boyfriend or side guy or whatever. All I want is to at least be able to call you my acquaintance, or my lover, or my friend, or something. I want to call you something, anything, sincerely, not my Joani or Siobhan, but an actual title for who you are to me."

"Why does it matter?"

"Because we're a little too close to just be strangers throwing caution to the wind. God, I feel like we have this fucking argument every other week."

"People fight," she still doesn't get it.

"Forget about it, I'm out," bye person.

"We're friends, ok?"

"No, if we're friends we should hang out once in a while and not worry that 'someone might see.' I mean the entire fucking neighborhood knows, I literaly have a parkingspace at the store with my name on it and you're worried that going out is goin' to raise some alarms."

"Really?"

"Yeah, Wayne did it. Sharpie but it's there."

"Who's Wayne?"

"The clerk."

"Now I can't tell if you're joking or not."

"It really doesn't matter, as childish as it may sound Joan, calling you my friend is important to me. So if you are please get dressed and lets go..."

"We're not that kind of friends... you should go," what other kind of friends are there?

"I don't want to leave you alone so long, but ok."

"He's going to be back in like two or three hours, it's no biggie," she sits back down on the bed.

"What's his name? And please don't say Max," I hug her from behind.

"No, it's Tyler. Why? And why can't it be Max?"

"I don't know bored, curious, too many Max's in the world."

"You're a pretty weird guy Jack."

"Yeah...I'm gonna go."

"Ok," I stand to dress and head for the door. I can't let this go, I need the last word, "just do me a favor and think about the people you do hang out with, how many of them are men and how many would you get a drink with and not worry about getting caught? Thank you. Goodbye!"

"Until next time!" she looks concerned, "Right?"

"Will there be a next time?"

"If you want," she's trying to shrug this off and play it cool. She's trying to be like me.

"Only if we really are friends," I take my leave, slamming the door.

What could I do? I really wanted to hang out with her. We've been seeing each other on Tuesdays, Thursdays, and Saturdays for two years now, recently we've established an open text policy because of her husbands' increasing absence. You don't just screw someone for a couple years and not want to spend some quality time with them; that would be sick and almost heartless.

**Thursday, The Rules**

Sorry if the random rules seemed out of place. There are quite a few things one must learn to keep this lifestyle going. A well-organized schedule is key to balancing your affairs; both in business and pleasure. Example: there are 168 hours in a week, 8760 in a year '84 in a leap year. The average person loses a third to sleep so that brings me down to about 5840 hours in an average year. Now take out my amorous affairs with seven regulars, nine occasional girls at about three and a half hours a pop gives us about 2580 to 2590 hours of fun leaving me with 3250ish hours left in my year and a majority of that goes to work in one form or another. Ain't math grand? You see what I mean about the importance of scheduling?

Now the nine occasional girls I have to make more intricate preparations for, they are already accounted for in my calculations but let's break down the logistics of the task at hand. I have a specific hotel that I reserve. I leave a key with the concierge and tell him or her that I am expecting a lovely young lady and give them a name and a brief description of her. To keep a low profile other than the initial text that reads *Here* by the girl I send only one message, a fake phone number as code, if the room is let's say 237 and we're meeting at 12:45 the text would read *508-237-1245* or something of that nature. It's simple, but it works. I then put a burner on the bed (I'm sure my local dollar store thinks me a drug dealer) and am never more than fifteen minutes away. It's real work I put into these meetings.

And speaking of work, I don't just have a balling Rolodex. No matter what you may think of me, it does contain all my work numbers too. Roughly eleven different business contacts: other bars, carpentry, mechanics, things I can do, you know. You do need a professional life, obviously. It can't all be about fucking.

There's not a book of laws to follow, everything I know and every rule I have I learned from experience. There are far more than five rules, but the rest are more or less in flux depending on the situation I'm in with each of my inamoratas, like rule thirteen pray she's superstitious not religious, religious women will either treat you like a scumbag or will start planning to leave their husband with the intention to marry, also there will probably be a priest in your neighborhood who she confesses to. Now with Thirteen I'm not saying only atheists are reliable, moderate, reformed, etc… are absolutely fine, I'm only talking about the extremely devout. So… for time let us stick with the five aforementioned rules, they're the real testaments to my survival. What's that old proverb 'out of chaos comes order' wait was that Nietzsche? I have learned how to have fun while surviving the fury of jealous husbands, boyfriends, and the occasional girlfriend. Not just surviving but thriving, whoever said you can't have your cake and eat it too? Then what the hell is the point of the cake?

Rule one: never go out together, this is the first one I learned, hence it being my number one. Picture lil'ol me a senior in high school with a junior named Emily, she was a short brunet with the bluest eyes I had ever seen, her reason for cheating you ask? She hated her boyfriend. We hung out, got chummy, had fun but she made it obvious, and to my discretion I wanted people to know too. I was proud. It's not that I cared about her in any romantic way, I did, however, feel a profound closeness. She was a good friend to me when Rachel left. She listened to me, and that's all I really needed. A few weeks into my psych sessions she confided in me that she needed an excuse to leave her beau. Her friends loved him, her mom loved him she just didn't. She placed her hand on my thigh, leaned in closer and kissed my cheek. I kissed her back and thing just escalated, I didn't know her boy toy nor did I want to hurt him I just wanted to help my friend. Em felt trapped and was willing to do anything she deemed necessary to escape. What's better than making him hate her, right? Well, Sunny Jim, it doesn't work that way.

Once, he found out he didn't blame her. This six foot one, two hundred and eighteen-pound pituitary case cold cocked me under the stairwell when I kissed Em good bye, remember what I said about guys turning into psychotic douches. The last thing I remember before the punch is her standing in the sunlight waving to me, the wind making ruffling her short hot pink skirt, sometimes I can still see that smile when I close my eyes while trying to sleep. I made it obvious, got reckless and didn't care until it caught up with me. I wrote this rule in the back of my first diary the second I got home.

Number two: always wear a rubber. This wasn't always my second rule. I shifted things around purely out of importance. I felt obligated to put this one near the top, if not for me then for future generations. Though I usually did wear condoms, especially in a one-night stand situation, I had made the mistake of trusting the girls I slept with regularly. After two catching the clap twice I made certain always to wear one, almost. Dartmouth, I was in Cats room when she got a call from her 'authoritarian boyfriend,' her words. She put on a movie to occupy my time while she went out on a date. Fifteen minutes into whatever anime dreck she put on her roommate came in, so surprised was she to find out that Cat was cheating because 'Eric is such a sweet guy.' Sorry, I don't remember her name so let's call her Amy. Amy and I in that time frame slept together, whether it was my charm, she hated her roommate almost as much as I did or she too submitted to the philosophy of 'why not' we thought soiling Cat's sheets more fun than the programing.

I didn't see Amy for like two or three weeks after our movie night and when I did she took me aside in the hall. I can still feel the panic I felt when I saw her hand gently touching her lower stomach when we first made eye contact, she was late. I am not proud of how I acted but I don't think I would change a thing. I gave her the A.O.A. talk (abortion or adoption). I can't imagine what went through her head. She disappeared after this, just faded away in the background. I don't even know if she kept it. So, there's a chance that a little me is in this world walking and talking and that scares the shit out of me. I am sorry about this, I was just doing what was best. This little faux pas forced me to make condom wearing my second rule.

It is important to know that there is nothing to what I do other than it's an art, it may be completely shallow but what form of commercial art isn't? Frist, you tend to lead an adventurous life but know these are all superficial encounters, all of them; they have to be in order to keep them going. One must be willing to live a solitary life and ready to let people go, I mean you have to keep moving and you can't with someone always around, which leads perfectly into my next rule, Emotions. You must avoid those that get too attached to you. They can hold you back, disrupt your life (dolls heads in the mail, that kind of shit) or will betray you in the end, once a cheat always a cheat. Remember that, write it down if necessary. I, early on in my career of making cuckolds, did fall for a young lass. She was a newlywed named Melody. I cared for her dearly, I would do anything she wished. I wanted her completely.

You see, I made a lapse in judgement thinking she felt the same, thinking that she was capable of feeling that deeply about anything. Long story short after her marriage fell apart and the opportunity for her to become mine opened I jumped into action relinquishing all my other lovers readying to settle down, she left me for someone else within a month. I had already bought a ring. There's a lot of fun here, but no more than there is pain. It is best if you intend to live like me to avoid emotions all together. Feelings, the feels, they lead to sloppy work, and sloppy work leads to higher chances of getting hurt or worse getting caught.

Rule four, egress. Do I need to recap the Providence fire escape scenario from earlier? Didn't think so. There are many examples in which this little tenet has come in handy but make sure he doesn't catch a glimpse of you as you leave or else you might wind up with a gun (or the flat side of a D battery) pressed against the back of your head with the guy pissed as hell whispering in your ear, 'You are scum. You are going to stop seeing Darleen. You are going to walk to your car and you will never come near my home or my woman again. Do you understand?' The only reason that I now know it was a battery was because he whipped it at me as I walked to my car, it hit my kidney and I pissed blood for a little while afterwards. Anyway, have a good escape plan.

Finally the fifth rule, the strangest and most polite of all rules, if any of these may be called such. Never promise anything to the guy, I may be an asshole that bests in skullduggery, but I won't lie if I'm directly confronted, I take pride in my honesty. I will look a man in the eye and say 'Yes, I am having sex with your girl,' shake his hand and compliment his taste. Back in college during my sophomore year, not Cat, an econ major named Sophia. She and I met in a group, and when the herd dwindled down to her, her roommate and me I suggested we go to my place. I was about to put on a movie (a vamp flick) when her roommate bailed, alone we watched the movie but didn't fully get into it, we started fooling around.

I pretended to be a vampire and every few seconds went after her neck, she would clench and giggle, make a cross with her fingers and I'd back away hissing. She stretched her neck giving me full access and I took it, she let me gnaw and kiss to my hearts' content so long as she could do the same and that I wouldn't kiss her on the lips. Kissing and nibbling quickly turned to feeling up and then we started dry humping. Her necklace caught my chin and I began to bleed, this lovely little nut fancied the iron-rich taste of blood, and well I was into the kink, letting her lap it off my face so long as I could touch her breasts. I thought it was a good evening and she left with a satisfied smile, then immediately told her boyfriend about our couch ride. He was not amused.

She and I continued to flirt via text, she stole my number from her boyfriends' phone. Before you think me a bigger asshole than you already do let me clear things up. He and I weren't friends; I had no amiacable or fraternal obligation to him. The only reason he had my number was that I offered to tailor his clothes when we first met, that is it. Incidentally, that was also how the night of the bloody couch ride started. She and I flirted for about a week until she wanted to meet up. I went to her dorm complex and stood outside blasting Van Morrison's 'Moon Dance' on my phone waiting for her. She stepped out, swayed with me for a sec, told me to shut off the music and took me down to the basement.

We stood in this white room just before the laundry area, there was this weird dilapidated chair coated in loose strands that I took, we just talked. She wanted to be friendly and talk literature, I am a fan of Oscar Wilde, and she had finished reading The Picture of Dorian Gray, so I was open to the conversation which quickly became a discussion of hedonism. The undertone was what she wanted and felt she deserved, I was in no position to argue so I came up with some plain reason to go to my room. I asked if she wanted to listen to my record player and continue dancing, she agreed.

In my room, we began dancing to what I think was my best of Bob Dylan record, if not then it was one of my Sinatra's. She got tired and sat on my bed as did I, quickly there was petting and nibbling, thing progressed rather quickly and the next thing I knew I took off her panties, threw her legs over my shoulders and began eating her out. We didn't have actual sex this night. When she came, or at least was close, I stopped and she began to cry, I freaked out. I kept apologizing and asked if she felt I took advantage of her. She told me no and said she was trying to be good this time. I sat with her for around an hour that night holding her close and letting her cry it out, as she left I asked if I may have a kiss.

We flirted still for a few days. The night I finally got to sleep with her was the night that her little leprechaun approached me, not knowing what she and I just did. I was having dinner alone in this the little restaurant on campus, it was like an hour or two after we screwed when Ray-Ray Amerson (not his real name) walked up to me. This man stood a towering five foot two with feathered copper hair, a chinstrap, and glasses, wearing a flannel button down over a white-T, a dark red leather jacket and khakis. He was quiet and distant, understandably of course, his hands were in his pockets, and for a moment I thought he was palming a switch blade. He removed his flat cap, threw it in the booth and took the seat across the table.

"Hey," he lifted his glasses and rubbed his eyes.

"Hello there Ray-Ray."

"How have you been?"

I stayed quiet, probably a bad sign but I was kind of deer in headlights staring into his beady eyes.

"You know it's not cool what you did, right?" I didn't know what he knew given that the first time stuff happened Sophia told him right away, I didn't want to incriminate myself, so I played it cool.

"I can't change the past and wouldn't if I could."

"But you can cause a lot of damage with your actions. You know this, right? You can ruin relationships, lives even," blowing it a little out of proportion, aren't we?

"So?"

"How is that supposed to make me feel around you?"

"I guess bad, I don't know. That's your prerogative."

"Has anyone ever told you that you have the personality of a sociopath?"

"Many, why do you ask?" I just smiled at him.

"Do you care at all?"

"No," I grabbed a napkin to wipe my mouth, "and here's why, you're not someone I actually know. We're not close, I met you like once or twice."

"But I'm human, same as you, can't you at least respect that?" I'm human? Since when?

"Existing doesn't earn you my respect. You actually have to prove you deserve it."

"Ok," he looked down, sighed, then readjusted himself, sitting upright, "so I'm not going to threaten you or hurt you, I'm just going to ask that you don't let it happen again and we can move past it."

"I'm not going to promise that," I wiped my mouth again as I finished my meal, he dropped his posture, arms crossed, resting on the table.

"Why?" he began whining at this point.

"Listen, I could lie to you and say that I'm sorry I'll never do it again blah-blah-blah but that's not who I am. I will say I currently have no intentions to escalate anything, but she's a consenting adult I'm a consenting adult if stuff happens stuff happens there's not much you can do, I'm sorry you're in this situation, but I'm not going to lie to you, can't you respect that?" I might have been an asshole, but at least I can say I never lied to him.

That meeting with Ray-Ray is not uncommon in my profession, for me, it's happened a few times with other heartbroken boys who think they can talk this out. All end the conversation by asking 'why do you do this?' I too have occasionally wondered that for someone just starting out with a taken girl the answers simple 'it's fun.' There is no want or reason other than it's exciting and you get the best side of the girls; you see their passions, their desires, and only have deep conversations, since time is always a factor there is never room for bullshit. You must learn to communicate a lifetime of stories in body language and whispers. The terrible fact is comfort stifles ones' ability to relay anything to another person, they always think they have more time than they do. But with me, they know exactly how long we have. An hour with Siobhan or Michelle and I know more about their innermost thoughts than their partners.

All true relationships start with lies. Minor things that you don't think twice about but at the end of the day still aren't the truth. A person who wants to impress someone will claim that they like a specific band, food, movie or some other stupid thing that in reality they may be indifferent to or hate, but will still make those claims and deal with the inconvenience to improve their chances of getting with their crush. The initial dishonesty might not even be verbally communicated; it could be silence on a subject so any political view, fetish, pet ownership, idea, opinion, sexy clown suits, etc... that isn't disclosed before the first time you sleep together is still being dishonest.

The reason you won't just come out and say your strangest fetish on the first date is obvious, you are afraid. You're afraid that you won't be accepted for being who you are. There's never a fear of loss with me because in the eyes of my girls my existence is solely to fulfill their every desire, any emotional gratification is incidental. I answered the why question to Ray-Ray and still give the same answer today when someone confronts me.

"I do this because it gives me a purpose. I bring joy to others just by being myself. Who am I but the guy whose name your girl calls out when you're not around?"

The funny thing about Ray-Ray is that we traveled in close-knit groups, we knew almost the exact same people so as I was screwing his girlfriend one day I would see him at a gathering the next. We did have a very close mutual friend, James Roth, who was once sent to talk to me or so I assume for he asked how things were with Sophia early in our conversation.

"She's alright, why are you asking me? She's got a beau?"

"Ray's not doing well man, you really fucked him up."

"No body's forcing him to stay with her."

"Dude...Come on."

"Hey, you are two of a kind."

"What?"

"You only see the small picture, you guys just can't see it from my perspective."

"And you're all-knowing."

"Well yeah... he's blinded by emotion, and you only know what's happening from word of mouth, particularly his."

"Why don't you enlighten me on your perspective of the Sophi-situation?"

"Gladly, I'm doing him a service." James face contorted in a way that screamed 'Bullshit', "Stick with me here. I'm doing him a favor. Best case scenario she and I stop, he feels like he's won his woman back and she'll appreciate him for being so understanding. Worst case they break up, he looks for someone who won't cheat on him 'cus he'll be wise to that shit, she has fun until she finds someone else suitable for the role of boyfriend and I get my dick wet," his eyes opened wide, "the only reason he's in pain is because he is trying to rationalize this or some stupid shit, let it go and it'll sort itself out."

"Wow," he was impressed that I actually put thought into my argument.

"If you can poke one hole in my reasoning, I will stop, but it can't be a moral argument that shit's always subjective."

"Well..."

"Just one flaw right now."

"Just... you just."

"Yes?"

"Fuck...Goddamn you're going to be a good lawyer."

"You too buddy, you too."

The relationship I had with Sophia lasted about two months, she was a love though, a natural cuddle bug and I think she actually cared about me. When I had a head cold, she ran over to my place with a jar of honey for my tea. I eventually stopped texting her because I fell for someone else. She knew I liked someone else and started to become possessive, mind you, she was still with Ray-Ray and was mad at me, the other guy, for developed feelings for another girl. I didn't think it was right fooling around with Sophia while chasing something serious with another girl.

Now back to reality, I wish that Siobhan would hang out with me now and then. To me, the weird thing is that she's the one who insists on classifying what we have as a 'friendship' but never wants to hang out. I would be fine if she thought of me just as a living vibrator always at her beckon call, something that she can do anything with, but that's not the case. She needs more than a good roll in the hay; she needs just enough of a connection to justify every text, every kiss, and every cuddle but any more and she fears that she'll be lost. Joani in some way still loves her husband but not enough to want to stay with him, what confuses me is that she doesn't resent him enough to leave.

She knows if she left I would be there to help, I wouldn't have to think about it, and I think she probably would if she was sure that I would be devoted to her and her alone. That I can't promise. She is a wonderful person, I can't stress that enough, and I care for her deeply, more than I should. She talks to me, not many people do; she asks me what I want. What do I want? I want her, I want to see her smile, I want to be there when she does, I want to see her tell the truth, I want her to tell me what she wants, I want to see her gagged and tied to a chair mounted on a powerful double penetrating vibrator covered in sweat, eyes bursting out of her head, breathing heavily and quaking in the lulls between her explosions of ecstasy, I want to see and hear her orgasm over and over and over again, I want to cuddle her, above all I want her to be happy.

I get why she would call me a friend: we text little jokes constantly, share personal things and even talk on the phone, she's one of two people I willingly call. Apparently that's a big deal. If we hung out at all I would revoke my hesitance and call her my friend. Maybe even my best friend. I just wish that I had someone to hang out with, you know? Of course, hence our conversations. Anyway, I still want to have a drink and do something.

**Thursday,7 pm, On the Dot**

Yes at times I can be a bar fly, not a big drinker myself at least not anymore, but it's something to do, and there are always people to meet. When a person has a few under their belt, think they'll never see you again, they become the most direct people in the world and hold nothing back. I appreciate that type of honesty, it's quite refreshing. I entered what I call the F.U.C. pub, (Fag Under Cross) it's a bar off of County, not a dive but nowhere near high end. It's just a place that can mix a drink, and I have work in a few hours so this could be my last chance to relax for a while. The best part is that I can see how tonight's gonna be, see the people who are out and about. Since it's well past the first of the month, welfare hasn't been mailed yet, it might be a slow night.

Sorry, I completely breezed over why I call it the F.U.C. The owner of this establishment is an old school Catholic, look over there at the big ass cross on the wall, the one with a picture of Pope John XXIII, well look a little closer. Under the cross, though it's been painted over you can still see the outline of a cartoonish cock (a rooster) carved in the wall. Before it was covered someone, i.e. Luke, carved the word 'Fag' in its elongated neck during his bachelor's party. Drinking a Black Russian, my phone goes off, sorry about this, it's Siobhan *I'm so sorry I was a jerk, I don't want you to be mad at me. Of course, we're friends.* I half way want to send back *Go suck an egg* but I won't, the best thing for me to do is to not respond for like a day, make her squirm maybe get a 'date' out of it or at least a scotch on the rocks, a little anniversary gift to myself. I know she'd do the same to me. And speaking of gifts, take a look at that beauty reading *'Dante's Inferno.'* I love girls with straight black hair, glasses, and brains. Her mode of dress is semi-formal, all black: a button-down with the sleeves rolled up a quarter of the way, her top three buttons undone showing the slightest hint of cleavage, her skirt hits right at the knee, I love her stockings they have some floral lacy design that looks quite seductive. Her shoes are shined heels that ride midway up her calf, her legs are crossed, and she's bobbing her right foot up and down.

When someone goes to a bar and sits alone at a small table with their nose in a book, you can tell that just being out of the house is practically a chore. They do it because that's what people do. Self-isolation; hiding behind a book to deter unruly prospects. What do you think? Is she with work friends, waiting on a blind date? Or does she just want to have a drink without anyone hitting on her? She's sitting at a small table that can at most hold four seats if no one orders food, I doubt work friends but maybe just a friend? No, why would she have a book? The book is a distraction. Wish me luck my friend.

"In the middle of the journey of our life, I found myself within a dark woods where the straight way was lost," she puts the book down staring daggers at me, her mouth is partially agape.

"You just *Goo-Gal-Tha-T*?" pronouncing Google as Goo-Gal her tongue flails sloppily as she over emphasizes the consonants in the last half of her speech.

"Dante's inferno. Classic."

"Yeah…" she squints her eyes slightly nodding her head with a sarcastic smile, "that doesn't answer my question," I sit down.

"*Amor, ch'al cor gentile ratto s'apprende…* yes I've read it, both in English and its native Italian."

"Impressive," she rolls her eyes.

"I'm sorry if I'm bothering you I just love the inferno."

"Then go join a book club."

"I would, but the last one I joined turned out to be a front for a cult. I mean, I would have stayed but after I sullied their sacrificial virgin they asked me to leave."

"Cute," a chuckle, that's a start.

"I find his damnation of the corrupt members of the papacy leading to his excommunication solely responsible for the books fame. All in all, it is a fairly dry text," she closes the book and looks at the cover.

"I like it so far," she's listening to me, hallelujah.

"You do."

"I mean I don't really understand what he's saying but it's interesting," she leans in a little, elbow on table, and perches her chin on her hand. She wants me to know she's not an expert, but she's trying.

"It's a long ass poem written in Italian and translated into English, most don't understand what he's saying," she smiles, she's at ease now, "but most also don't finish the trilogy, it's always the Inferno, never Purgatorio or Paradisio. Which leads me to question 'is it really pleasing because of its content?' or do you just like that so few people read it. I mean the appeal is that it's both esoteric and renown. It makes you feel smarter than the dullards that don't know what you're talking about but know the title that you're so versed in. I find self-applause, next to sex, to be the greatest motivation."

"I'm sorry but was there a question in there?" moment of comfort gone, she so wants to call me an asshole.

"Rhetorical one somewhere, yeah. My point is the history of Dante and what this book did to him is far more interesting than the book itself."

"Yeah I'll keep that in mind," she picks the book back up.

"I'm sorry if I offended you, that was not my intention."

"It's fine," she flips the page in an exaggerated manner.

"No, it's not. Full disclosure, as a single guy in a bar we are petrified to talk to women. Even just to talk literature. We come off as awkard or aragant."

"Or both."

"Yes!"

"Poor you."

"Come on, imagine you're a guy going up to a young lady in a bar, such as yourself, what would you think their first thought is? Obviously 'I'm being hit on,' right?"

"You know it."

"I'm really screwing this up. I just saw you reading a book I very much admire and thought it would be fun to talk about it. Quoting, in my opinion, was just a nice way to start the conversation and introduce myself," she ignores me. "Look, I'm sorry for bothering you, I'll leave," she looks up as I stand and then back to the book.

"But the stars that marked our startling fall away…"

"We must go deeper into greater pain."

"Wow, you actually memorized this thing."

"Practically, cantos are easy."

62

"Compared to what?"

"Chapters, I don't know. I wanted to sound clever," this won't go anywhere, a little banter with a hostile partner, I'm not going to press on. "Have a good night."

"Hey!" she calls me back, I ignore her. This isn't me playing hard to get, she rubbed me the wrong way so I'm out. I can feel her eyes burning through me, those dark spheres of rejection tearing into my chest like a deer slug. I need to have another Russian.

I'm sorry. I was hoping that I could demonstrate how a proper introduction and conversation can lead to a romantic evening, I got too cocky and it backfired. Back at the bar, some old guy is sitting down next to my chair. Check my coat, yep still have my wallet. Good thing you're imaginary 'cus damn he reeks, either he's a fisherman or that's some awful B.O. He's old but has a new wedding ring, how can a woman fall in love with that stench? Has to be money, he's a fisherman.

"How is it out there? They biting?" making my inquiry.

"It's goin', they're bitin'…is it really that obvious?"

"Guy you reek, there ain't no kind way to say it. You're either a fisherman or knee deep in bad clams."

"Bad clams?" as he asks, I look back at the girl still sitting alone head tilted down glaring at me from under her glasses mouthing 'what the fuck?' not wanting to cause greater conflict I quickly look back to my man.

"You know," I slack into my stool, "vag." I whisper, "hey buddy, I'm Jack," I give him my hand to shake.

"Max," mother fucker, I have hit my maximum tolerance for the name Max today.

"You married there, Max?"

"Why?" he snarled, turning his head to look at me, one eye partially closed, his face dried and tanned, wrinkles to spare. There is a lot of grey in his scruff. I can't stop looking into his milky blue eyes, full of sorrow but that heavy brow shows nothing but anger. His clothes, covered in mud, blood and holes, look as though he's had them for the past decade.

"Just curious," I wave my hands in defense.

"Why?" sensitive, she's either in it to win it, or he suspects her cheating. Well, Maxie, I was plowing this chick earlier and her husband came home trying to find out who she's been fucking on the side. His name is also Max, so... I figured it's kind of a co-inky-dink.

"No reason, start a conversation."

"Piss off, boy," strike right to my pride. Now I comfort myself in the thought that I might be screwing his wife. And balance is restored, I look down to my drink nod my head and breathe calmly.

"Ok sir, I was trying to be nice but ok."

"Hey, hey Mic," to the bartender, "Mic cut this asshole off."

"What, you're trying to get me eighty-sixed?" I'm so going sixty-nine on your bitch, "Fine asshole. Michael, you needn't cut me off I'll leave the guy alone."

"Nah, Mic, eject the fucker," the fisherman interjects, Mic looks at me and shaking his head, I pull out my wallet.

"Shut it you sour old bastard," I throw down eight dollars, look back, wave to the reader and as I leave box the old guys' ear.

That fucking guy. All I wanted to do is have a drink, listen to some tunes and converse. That too much to ask? Trying to relax and the first girl I say 'hi' to chews me out like I'm shit. 'Oh, all I want is to fuck you?' yeah sure, but at least I wasn't acting like a complete dick. I gave her some credit for having good taste. Goddamn, you can't be nice to people round here. It's a fucking army of assholes and prudes ready to burn free agents like myself at the stake. Riddle me this, because I hear old timers constantly complain about the young, how is our generation supposed to learn respect when our elders are all pricks? When you make euthanasia seem like an attractive concept you have failed at resembling anything worth reverence. What should I expect, the people here are all the same.

Don't you think he was completely out of line?

Hold up, I gotta take a piss. I walk down the alley behind the bar and drain the lizard, I hear the door creaking and slam. I jump a little, get some on my shoes. I have to hurry up and... and... done. I turn to walk to my car, a shadow standing at the opening of the alley, it charges at me. Fucking Max. The nerve of this guy, he's got the fuse of a real Potugi, and you can't reason with a mad one. He tackles, lifting me off the ground. I punch him in the back of the head twice bringing him down. We slide a good three feet on the gravel. My side is killing me, he must have cracked a rib or something.

I roll on top of him; punch his nose as hard as I can, the blood is a nice effect, it's gushing. You can hear the gurgling as it flows down his throat and he struggles to breathe. He frees himself by catching me in the eye, hard enough to knock me off but no blood. He gets on top of me, the blood rains on my face as he wraps his fingers around my throat. He's not just choking me, he's strangling. Cutting the time of consciousness I have in half. I think of Jule. I've been in enough fights to know not to panic it eats up more oxygen. That flailing you see me doing isn't me fighting him off it's me trying to find something. A rock, well a large piece of brick. I smack him across the face with it, he falls off of me and tries to run away. Still with the rock, I whip it at his knee, that snap sounds promising. On the ground he turns to me holding a Swiss army knife scooting backwards, I check my side. (Side note, if Switzerland is neutral then why do they have an ARMY knife?) My shirt has a sliced on the torso just under my armpit, I poke through the hole, fresh blood. He sliced my ribs.

"God fucking damn it, this is my favorite shirt!" I walk up to him, he points the knife at me shaking. I kick it out of his hand, he pulls his arms in covering his head. Pathetic. I curb stomp his junk, and he falls over, my rage cools.

"Fish fucker what's your deal with me?" he puts his arms down.

"You're a punk," he's groaning out the pain.

"And you're a salty old bastard in dire need of an ass kicking, your point?" he say nothing, just cradling his genitals tapping his feet against the ground.

"Max, I'm goin' to walk. I suggest you do the same."

"And if I don't?"

"Well with a bum leg and no knife I think it'd be a pretty one sided fight. And I'd say my foot's goin' to be your dildo for the night, you read me?"

He sits back up propping himself against the wall, "yeah Mo, I read you," you calling me a 'Mo'? Seriously? There can't be this many Max's in the state.

"You calm?"

"Yeah I'm cool."

"No, I didn't ask if you're cool I asked if you were calm. I'm not getting out of your face till I know you're calm," I take a step closer to him.

"I'm calm, I'm calm," I take two steps back.

"Good, now you're not gonna want to put any weight on that leg, it's gonna hurt like a bitch."

"Ok," I walk to the wall of the building next door and lean on it.

"You ain't gonna sucker punch me now, are you?"

"What would be the point?" he's out of breath, wheezing, I hate that annoying whistle coming from his nose. "Cigarette Maxi-pad?" I pull the pack out of my jacket and slide one out, he shakes his head no. "Suit yourself."

"I'm sorry."

"Oh, fuck you!"

He looks down, quiet. He's so fucking pitiful. Damn it; death wish, doesn't caring about the pain he's in, his ring isn't new it's polished. His wife just died.

"Last name?"

"Huh?"

"What's your last name?"

"Rodriguez."

"Spanish?"

"Port-Spanish mix used to be Souza."

"Where the hell did you get Rodriguez?"

"Mom, where do think?" wait a minute. No fucking way.

"Hey, really random question did you ever teach at Roosevelt?" I flick my cigarette into a nearby puddle. I don't know if it's blood, oil, water, or piss.

"How you know that?" what are the odds? I'm jumping in excitement.

"Wooo, fuck… God, it's a small world. Fuck! Coach, it's me Jack, Jack Fabbrico. Last year you worked before the

Raunch blew it all away. When did they let you out you dirty old man?"

"I was only in jail a little over two years."

"Uh-hu uh-hu, so whacha been doing with yourself ol'rapey?" I can't help myself. It's been too long and too many laps.

"You're really asking for an ass kicking," with that gimp leg? Really?

"Hey old man, I think I already proved I can take you," I do a little shadow boxing to taunt him.

So we sat down in the gutter, he pulled a rag out of his pocket and handed it to me to wipe the blood off my face, and then we just talked. He told me that he moved around a lot taking whatever jobs didn't reject him immediately after discovering his status as a sex offender. He changed his last name hoping it would help, spoiler alert it didn't. Nobody told him that businesses do background searches via social, so it doesn't matter what you call yourself. When you change your name there's a paper trail, you just wind up appearing guiltier than if you were to embrace what happened. I mean not only do you look guiltier but extremely incompetent in hiding from your past, if he admitted he made a mistake he might have gotten a job sooner. He eventually became a truck driver for a couple of years mainly carrying fruits and vegies through the south and occasionally carried a load cross country.

I found out I was right in my first deduction, new bride and a youngin' ta boot. When he was sent up here, he met and fell in love with a very young woman in some snack shack (I made an inappropriate joke about going there, he got mad and refused to tell me her name when I asked). Thankfully she was legal when they married, that much he did say. I might have provoked him to have to clarify with a little taunting.

He married her as quickly as possible; he says because he loves her, I think he fears no one will look past the statutory. He moved back here when he got a job at a fishing company, finally making some decent money.

One mistake ruined his life and he had to start from scratch with a hundred pound restraint attached to his legs. That's not fair, is it? A century or two ago someone would have been trying to marry off their twelve-year-old to a man in his thirties. Juliet was like twelve or thirteen in Shakespeare's play, Desdemona was significantly younger than Othello. I know for a fact that Raunchy had tits back then and that she came onto him. Shit... he was blown by Rachel, this prick was luckier than me.

Judge me not. I left coach in the gutter weeping. Nursing his busted leg and balls, I called him a cab and walked away. I left the alley to the main road looking for my car, I walk quite a distance. I guess in the skirmish I had forgotten where I parked, still a little dizzy from the lack of oxygen and blood rushing back to my head. I got all the way to the end of the street and turned back to the bar, fuck my life. I'm pretty pissed right now; my eye fucking hurts, my head is pounding and I'm bleeding, I'm not ready for work. I can hear the echoing of that sorry bastard bawling his eyes out. Keys... my keys, thank God, Allah, Yahweh, Zeus, Tesla whoever for keychain beepers. The lights flash four cars down. As I walk to my car, from the shadows Dante's bitch appears, please don't think I'm a creep or stalker. I pop my jacket collar and keep my head down to avoid being seen. If it weren't for her glowing eyes she would have blended in with the night, her tan skin and black clothes would camouflage her in that corner. She really is quite a beauty.

"Hey, hey!" I'm leaving. Let me alone, "guy!" I stop walking.

"I'm just leaving, ok. I lost my car for a minute, I really don't want trouble."

"I have something to say. Wait up," she walks towards me.

"Really please, I'll go."

"Why are you acting like I... what the hell happened to your eye?"

"It's fine, I'm fine."

"Come here let me see," she puts her hand on my face, I pull away.

"What are you doing? Don't touch me."

"It's ok I'm a C.N.A." that doesn't just give you the right to touch people whenever.

"I'm fine Miss, please don't."

"Grace."

"What?"

"My name's Grace. You just need ice. Come back inside."

"No, I'm ok. I'm gonna go," leave me alone.

"What's the matter with you? I'm trying to help," I say nothing and she continues to look at my eye. Please stop, I don't want to be touched, "just a bit red and a little swelling, mister?"

"Mark," aliases, always have a few at hand.

"Well, Mr. Mark I'm sorry I was a little short with you in there. That was rude of me."

"Who brings a book to a bar?"

"A lonely, lonely person waiting on a date that never showed. I'm sorry I thought you were this guy my friend's trying to set me up with and..."

"And you wanted to make a point, to make him feel bad for being late?"

"It's not the best plan."

"I think not," she looks behind me.

"Your car?"

"If I say no and you see me drive off with it I'm a liar, if I say yes I become infinitely less cool."

"It's nicer than mine," she's smiling at me. Who'd a thunk it? She actually has a kind smile.

"Look I rarely get a second chance to make a good first impression, but I really have to go now."

"Really?"

"Yeah, work. Go inside. Wait for your date."

"He's not coming," I see a guy standing near the door staring at her. A little young and doesn't know how to dress like an adult. Take off the fucking baseball cap. He takes a second and looks at his watch, I think it's the guy.

"You're too cute to reject."

"You're sweet," I so don't want to get into another fight, the guy is still staring at us please let me leave. The guy shakes his head and walks into the bar, I hope I didn't fuck up her night too bad.

"I'm sorry, but I'm really running late, have a good night."

"Wait, don't you want to exchange numbers or somethin'?" no, not at all. I open my door.

"You're waiting for someone. I really don't think that's appropriate."

"He might not come."

"Then again he might."

"I don't want to waste my night," she presses herself against me; on her breath I smell brandy and coffee liquor. I hate work.

"You never know, but if he truly is a no show and looking at you I truly believe he's just late, then come here tomorrow around seven thirtyish."

"You'll be here?"

"If he's really a no show, cross my heart and hope to die."

"What if he does come tonight? Am I not allowed to go tomorrow?"

"I shall bestow upon you the greatest wisdom of all my years on this planet 'you do you,'" she smiles.

"I like that," I brush the hair from her face.

"Good night Grace."

"Have a good night Mark," she kisses me on the cheek, I should have chosen a cooler name.

As I'm about to get into my car I hear a screech from the corner, I stand and close my cars' door and look around. I can't make out any of the cars features other than it's black and has four doors. The passenger; a young man in his late teens or early twenties, either Portuguese or Latino, wearing a do-rag and a wife beater, wielding a nine millimeter, firing it in the air, screaming at the top of his lungs. I look back to Grace.

"Get inside!" she sprints to me instead, idiot. She buries her face in my chest for protection. Since when am I bullet-proof?

"Mark," she whimpers.

I back out of her clutches, throw her over my shoulder and run her to the door. The car has already passed by, we're as safe as we can be here.

"Go inside," she grabs me by the shoulders and kisses me.

"You saved me."

"No, I just wanted to sneak a peek under your skirt. Now please go where it's safe, well safer than out here," she kisses me on the cheek several times before pulling me in for another passionate one, her fingers combing through my hair. Near death experience, always a panty peeler.

"I'll see you tomorrow?"

"Sure. It's a date," I hold her hand, and as gently as possible I lead it to my lips. "And speaking of dates, enjoy yours."

"Nighty night Mark," she walked back in with a big smile, pupil's dilated from the surge of adrenaline, not taking her eyes off me until the door closes completely. The perks of being a man of action, you always look sexy.

I believe our friend Dante said it best 'From there we came outside and saw stars,' there was a little magic in the tone of her voice as she hushed my guise. I got in my car and finally drove away. I did a good thing, right? I calmed her down, protected her, ran her to safety. That's good guy stuff, right? Her dates going to have a better night with her than he would've if she never met me, I mean she'd either be pissed or dead. Now they have something to talk about. Just being late doesn't automatically mean he's bad. Even if he is an asshole there are no prince Charming's in this world and if there were I'm far from being one. Hey, best case scenario she has a good night, falls in love, pushes out a few brats and lives a normal life. Worst case I have a date tomorrow. Red light, open phones calendar and set *Grace/FUC 730 DON'T BE LATE!!!!*. Green light, close the phone and go. I arrive at my building, it's eight thirty. Believe it or not, even after this day I still gotta beat off before I go to work.

**Thursday, 8:46pm, Getting Ready for Work**

Ok, ok, inviting you in my shower might be a little quick givin' that you just met me a few hours ago, but I'm just sharing every aspect of my life. And hey, buddy, keep your eyes up here, that's only for my prospects. Yes, I shave my chest, and no those cuts aren't from dull razors. My rib you ask? The cut wasn't too deep, but it still needed some minor attention; I scrubbed it out with alcohol. It wouldn't stop bleeding so I took a lighter to a big spoon and cauterize it, then pressed some ice to numb the burn. Afterwards I put the ice to my eye.

As you can see from my hygiene products, I am a simple man who still likes to take care of himself. My soap, nothing too overbearing, just a moisturizing body wash. I don't go for that Axe, Tag shit you want a subtle scent to smell like an adult. Also, hydrating washes make your body feel baby soft, that's how girls like their men nowadays. Floating somewhere between a lumberjack and a Victoria's Secret model. Sitting on the shower rod you can see I have a couple cleansers and face scrubs, all mildly scented of course, they're the only types I buy. You don't want some flowery herbal scent to combine with your cologne, or natural musk if you choose to go au naturel. I avoid conditioner altogether, my hair just comes out looking greasy. I do use shampoo, it's that strengthening herbal shit that's supposed to be good for the hair, no smell and I only use it every other day. My towels are just that, towels: cheap, monochromatic, and fairly plush for my delicate form.

My bathroom setup is common for this area. The floor is white with one by one-inch tiles. My sink, white porcelain covered in cracks and scratches, is in the shape of a seashell, currently it has a few ice cubes melting in the drain and a mirrored medicine cabinet hanging above. In the soap groove you see two tubes, one is a clay face mask, and the other is a daily moisturizer, both of which are to keep me looking young and *Purdy*. On the other side of the faucet, there is a dropper of knock-off No More Red Eye.

My room, the pentagon, is right outside the shower. It's relatively square, it would be a perfect parallelogram if it weren't for the two-foot wide fifth wall that takes the would-be corner on the left side of my bed. I keep a leather chair in that spot where the three windows meet; it's the rooms' main source of light and great for reading, the other light being the yellowish dome above head. This time of the year I tend to keep the small middle window open at all times. My bed, a queen, has no frame. I prefer to be low on the ground; you never lose anything under the bed and tend to get less noise complaints. I usually don't bring my playmates back here, their beds are just so much more comfortable, but there are a few exceptions and I gotta be a considerate neighbor when those moments arise. Now please let me step into my closet, you can come if you want.

My clothes: I work as a bouncer, occasionally bartender, so I don't have to be fancy. I have a flat black T, black jeans, belt with mace attached. Also, it is heavily recommended to wear a dog tag. 'Why?' you ask, because it makes people think I've had military training. That may sound stupid, but it does prevent a lot of fuckers from messing with me. And in case you're wondering, yes I do meet women on the job. Some girls are oh so grateful. I enjoy my work, for five and a half hours a day, three days a week, it pays pretty well not to mention the tips, and it is kind of fun. You have not lived until you've beat the ass of some shitfaced roid-raging douche yelling 'do you know who I am?' I love that line. The answer is always 'I don't care.'

Now the cologne, I don't go too expensive. You smell like a preppy asshole if you have a two hundred dollar bottle on your bureau and no one likes the smell of an asshole, but you can't smell cheap either. I have a good range of forty-five to sixty dollar colognes, just one squirt under the shirt and now one above.

Here comes my half hour drive to work. People, by which I mean Anne, tell me I need to work closer to home. She always says there are plenty of bars and clubs in New Bedford and Fall River that I could work at, I just look at her and say 'that hits too close to home for me.' I like where I work, it offers me more food options on the way home. It also gives me the motivation to spend the night at someone else's place and pretends I don't live in this shithole.

I love my place, don't mistake that. I love it all from the exposed brick to the dripping sink. The tall ceilings, the wire lights hanging down, my breakfast bar and the big ass windows in my living room, this place smacks of hipster. Sorry, I'm hungry, need a little something to eat. Cereal, I do love my Coco pebbles. This place is huge, and the rent is amazing, less than something half its size. I'll let you in on the little trick I used to get this place so cheap, research. Quite an interesting history this place has, in 87' someone was murdered in my living room, the killer then attempted to burn the place down. Mmmmm… chocolatey milk. You can't sell milk like this. There's nothing that comes close, it's just too good to recreate. The place was condemned until 91' when it was bought by, interestingly enough, the killers cousin. Since then the area has kinda gotten shitty. Everyone pretty much forgot about the murder but it's still on file, so I used it. Not many know buildings can suffer psychological damage too.

I look out my window. The moon peeks out of a pocket of clouds, a waning gibbous, I'd say about four fifths visible. The sky flashes with hot lightning. I look at the roads, they're dry as a bone, I hate the humidity. Damn I need to do dishes, no time, one more bowl shouldn't make a difference. Well, its' been nice evaluating my living quarters but now it's time for work. I shut off the lights and think for the first time since I moved here I'm actually appreciating this place. It's very me.

I'm almost there, I'm not going to say the name of the place I work 'cus you'll tell your friends and they'll tell theirs, and I'm left shooting down a dozen people saying something like "Yo, brah I totally know you. You're friends with Johnny, who knows Mikey who's the little brother of this chick Tara that I just boned behind the Chili's dumpster. It's like we're practically family." Anonymity is key to my sanity, the unknown holds no stress and no praise. I will, however, tell you that it's somewhere between Point Street and the heart Downtown Providence. That gives you around one and a half square miles maybe two to work with.

**Thursday, 10:00pm, Work Acumen**

"I too, as happens to every man once in his life,
have been taken by Satan into the highest mountain
in the earth, and when there, he showed me all the
kingdoms of the world, and as he said before, so
said he to me, 'Child of earth, what wouldst thou
have to make thee adore me?' I reflected long, for a
gnawing ambition had long preyed upon me, and
then I replied, 'Listen,—I have always heard of
providence, and yet I have never seen him, or
anything that resembles him, or which can make me
believe that he exists. I wish to be providence
myself."

-Alexandre Dumas, Chapter 48, *Count of Monte
Cristo*. This is my favorite excerpt.

This quote has always resonated with me in somewhat of
a profound way. He, the count, followed his wish to be
Providence by being judge, jury, and executioner to those who
took away the happy life that Edmond Dantès, the Count, could
have had. Dumas followed this passage by calling Providence a
beautiful and noble thing. Though nobility is laughable, I will
admit to this; the city of Providence, in early summer, has some
of the most beautiful nights I've ever seen. Not to mention the
fact that one of my favorite writers and master creeps, H.P.
Lovecraft, was born and buried here.

I hope you like comics 'cause things are about to get
nerdy; Lovecraft a Mass-Rhodey mix, like myself, wrote *The
Thing on the Doorstep* and had (allegedly) been inspired by
Danvers state mental hospital for the setting of the sanitarium in
the fictional town of Arkham Mass which then inspired the
Asylum in the DC Universe. That's just another thing that I love
about being here, the history; sure I might get beaten sensless, or
shot, or stabbed if I take more than sixty steps from this door but
the temperature is nice, the stars are bright, and the women
aren't bad looking, some you might even call pretty. This is just
a place of scumbags and whores, and though my candor may
taste you as judgement note that I'm not saying there's anything

wrong with those who live that life, hell I'm one of them. I am as the count wished to be, I am Providence incarnate.

You know a study was done which showed that the Providence area, which bleeds into and pretty much is Bristol County Massachusetts (my bread and butter), has the least honest people in the nation, seriously look it up. With unemployment almost two points higher than the national average everyone jumps on the poverty bandwagon to justify the shittiness of the people here. Though I, personally, find that to be a bullshit excuse for social apathy.

The argument of poverty as the cause of crime made by the socialites and politicians greatly contradicts Blake's philosophy that crime is an independent action and what are politicians supposed to be but versed philosophers. I am not a politician, and I have no interest in being one, however I like to think of myself as a philosopher. Maybe not versed but well-rounded to some extent. If I may again quote to prove how well-read I am, et hem…

"Want of money, and the distress of a thief can
never be alleged as the cause of his thieving. For
many honest people endure greater hardships with
fortitude. We must, therefore, seek the cause
elsewhere than in want of money, for that is the
miser's passion, not the thief's."
-William Blake

If I am reading this properly and my analytical skills aren't fully misguided, I would say a thief is not a homeless man or someone in need because the needy can ask for help appose to thieving. What's rotting this city is vanity, greed, and the lack of money. One can be happy and poor, one can be miserable and rich, but if a person has the desires and vanity of the rich and is placed in the situation of the poor then they must become criminals in order to satiate their sense of avarice. As you may be able to tell there is a lot of time on this job for me to mull over a few philosophers, poets, writers and really let it sink in.

With every free moment you have picked up a book, you never know who could be a fan. Regardless if you can use the knowledge to your advantage just having it is impressive and it will lead to long, deep, conversations down the line. Plus, you make a great first impression if you always come off well-read. But, my friend, if you're not heavy in the literary world then go cinema; classic, foreign or independent, film is the art of the modern man, so be versed.

I'm not going to call what happened earlier with Grace supportive evidence, because I didn't close the deal. Though it would have been easy to get her in bed by the end of our encounter it wouldn't have been me getting her in the mood, it would have been the rush of adrenaline and in my book that's not fair. Now if I staged the shooting to make myself look the part of a hero, then that would be a different story.

I get paid fairly well here; by that I mean just enough for rent and food. As I've said I have a 'plethora' of freelance jobs, other bars, and some carpentry but lately I haven't been accepting calls. You know, tips from jag-offs that want to be with the cool people really adds up. The average guy is willing to pay up to fifty bucks to get in, (but if I'm going by averaging it's more like forty bucks a pop) so long as they aren't too hideous and dress properly I can look the other way now and again, but only a few a night, you need a cut off number to be sure you won't get caught letting in the wrong people. So... can't let in more than fifteen people that are fives and sixes a night and I split that with my partner. Then we must spread our seven or eight over the shift to reduce the chance of someone noticing what we're doing. We split the profit down the middle, so it doesn't matter if I let in eight or he does. More fun with math: fifty times seven and a half times three... that's just over an extra grand a week, note I am going by averages. It's about twelve fifteen right now, I'm covering the door by myself and have already made almost three hundred dollars.

Shawn, my partner, is behind the building with his prick in some chicks' ass telling her to squeal like a little piggy, he's kinda going through a 'Deliverance' phase, but that's how desperate some people are just to be with the 'In' crowd. I can't say anything against him, except for the anal... gross. I do the same thing; use my power of influence to get what I want, usually a name and number, and maybe a kiss after a long conversation. You see if you demand sex you might just get it but it's definitely a one-time type deal, and it's not as much fun, in my opinion, if it's demanded. Just seeing you again will make the girl remember she's whore. But being a charming, charismatic gentle man, well… they get repeat business, and you both leave with happy memories. And guy it's fine to have types but don't look for idiots to fill your contacts, once the physical pleasure is over what are you left with? An idiot. You'll listen to the same annoying stories over and over again, she might not take birth control, won't know much in the boudoir, and if she has a beau, her affair would be half-assed which at best will be endangering your safety at worst your reputation. So please unless it's a one-night stand no dumb asses.

Everything you think you know about bouncers is probably right or pretty close. We are the judges of the establishment, looking solely at aesthetics. I know what I do is unfair. I say who is and isn't right for the party based entirely on appearance alone, but what's better? If f'ugly over there feels complete because someone, i.e. me, whose opinion shouldn't matter to him, pretends that he's cooler than the other side of the pillow. An act that inevitably would cause the desired clientele to leave, losing money for this business or destroy his selfesteem and keep the few people in this town that actually work employed? It's my duty as a humanitarian to reject that dweeb. I'm a necessary evil.

"Hey Poindexter: Clearasil, lose the flannel and buy some wearable clothes then you'll get in, God, are you trying to make me sick? Go home," he's a crier. Why do the criers always come when there's no one here to enjoy it with? I love my job so much. "Out of my face. Now!" I push his shoulder, and he sprints away, he even runs with a certain dopey awkwardness. Shawn comes back. Good, you get to meet Shawn. Yeah, I know he smells like vag and swamp ass, but he is one of the best got darn bouncers in this town.

"Hey, you just missed another crier."
"I think I had a little more fun, what was he wearing?"
"Tan khakis and a flannel jacket."
"Shirt?"
"Black T."

"My God, it's like he's trying to get thrown out."

"I know right. You're in."

"Was he a hipster type?"

"Nah, just a geek."

"Did you chew him out?"

"Sort of, told'em what he did wrong."

"You're too kind sometimes, you got to really let them have it. You make this place harder to get into the more they want in. God look at the ass on that one," he practically blows it a kiss.

"I was staring at her friends' tits."

"Man, I wanna stick that peach."

"You want everyone's ass."

"I wouldn't make you my piggy bitch."

Shawn is probably the closest thing I've had to a real friend in a few years. We met when I first started in the bar scene, he's the one who got me this job. March 26th, I turned twenty-one, my sis took me out to celebrate. As the night wore on so did her patients. The entire day I got blitzed, and she got bitched. We started at the F.U.C. way back when the original owner had authority then hopped around between fast food joints, liquor stores, and dive bars. We started to bicker, and she eventually abandoned me either in the third or fourth bar we went to. We might have gotten into a disagreement and I may have made a comment on the endless benefit that her being barren will have on society as a whole, do in part to the fact that her emotional temperament would be better suited for an iceberg than raising a child, me being the prime example. In far less sophisticated word obviously. I was, of course, pretty shitfaced.

I was getting cut off around one-one thirty, the tender took my keys, and I had no money for a cab. I pleaded with the bar-lacky when Shawn raised his hand and said: "I'll take him home." He was just some guy at the counter hitting on every chick that came by, so pretty good by my standards. He was cool even when rejected; if a girl wasn't into him, he would just shrug it off say 'that's ok' and return to his drink. 'You sure' the tender asked me, I'm shit faced do you really expect me to have an opinion?

"He offered me a ride?" I asked.

"Yeah."

"Cool," I stood and wobbled towards the other end of the bar slipping on some vomit, I don't think it was mine. I hugged the stool and pressed my forehead to the cold textured steel leg and closed my eyes. I was nudged awake, and a hand was presented to me.

"You alright?"

"Fine and dandy Randy," he helped me up onto a seat.

"Shawn."

"Peter Pan."

"What?"

"Nothing. Don't mind my mouth talk," I lay my head on the counter facing him. "Is it night-night time?"

"Close to it. I see your lady friend left."

"That wasn't a lady, that was my sister."

"Aw. Close family, cute."

"No, not really. She's a bitch usually."

"Well you're in my company now, I just want one thing."

"A puppy!" I shouted.

"Can you promise you won't puke in my car?" I sat up.

"You know I can promise you anything, but I'm not sure if I can deliver. Oooh let's get pizza," he laughed.

"I'm not feeling food right now, but let's get you home."

"M-kay."

When the tender rang the closing bell, Shawn walked out practically carrying me on his shoulders. His car was what I, in my state, believed to be a brand new red corvette z06 which I was freaking out over, but in reality was an 04' bright orange Mitsubishi Eclipse. That might have appeared a little crazy to him especially when I hugged/dry humped it. This is just to give you a clue into my mental state at the time. We sat in his car for a while, I drifted in and out of consciousness throughout the ride.

"Wha'chu do?" he asked, waking me.

"Does it make a difference?" I think that's what I said.

"Yeah, if I'm driving a millionaire I feel I have the right to know it?" I dozed off again.

"Hey, hey. Wake up."

"What we here?"

"No, you just passed out. I don't know where I'm going."

"New Bedford I'm in there somewhere."

"We're in New Bedford. Where?"

"Oh, I don't know. Do you know where Oakas Pizza is? I'm on that street. Hey, want pizza?" I was at that time living with Anne and Luke.

"No, I'm goin to go to bed."

"Fun-fun."

"Hey, you never said what you do?"

"Bitches," I started laughing hysterically.

"Man rated S, savage."

"Brilliant."

"You like it? It's yours. I meant for money."

"Bitches," he chuckled a little too this time, "nah, I do weird shit, I am kind of a handy man. You know like a mister fix it."

"Pay well?"

"I live with my sister and couldn't pay for a cab, what do you think?"

"Do you want a job?"

"I ain't gay."

"You're funny, no I mean have you ever been in a fight."

"First rule of cight flub you do not do gay shit."

"Want to be a bouncer? We need a new guy to help me work the door."

"You just met me."

And that was six years ago; he got me hired here, trained me and talked me up to be an on call bartender. Shawn has saved my ass more times than I can count. I can't thank him enough, without him I'd probably be dead or worse still living with Anne.

"Why with the pig squeals?" I have to know.

"Deliverance, you know Burt Reynold, Ned something and John…"

"I know the movie, but I have to know. Is that really a turn on? Go in," a young lady quietly passes by and I think she took a little bit of my heart with her, well at least a portion of my

81

attention. I tune out Shawn for a sec and watch her go in. I love black hair and glasses. She's about a seven but could pass for a nine in the right light, clothes, and makeup, I'd do her.

"I'm sorry, what'd you say?"

"I said sometimes, sometimes it's a dominance thing. You're in," a guy just did the high five-slide, and slipped him two twenties.

"Kay Marquis, if you want a good ass fucking scene in a movie 'Last Tango in Paris' just add butter."

"Nah, I can't watch that shit."

"Why not?"

"I don't speak French."

"It's not all in French."

"Good amount is."

"How would you know?"

"Tried watching it once."

"Then put on the subtitles."

"Then I'm not watching a movie, I'm reading one. You, hell no!" another dweeb, about five foot five with frosted tips. This is not 1998, go back to your fucking boy band.

"Ok then don't watch it, at least look up the butter scene."

"Nope," he's laughing a little.

"Why? In, stop, you in, you back of the line," three girls: one of which is obviously a perspective enhancer for the other two. A perspective enhancer is a befriended ugly person used to make their *Friends* look better by comparison, not that the other two are ugly or amazing looking, they just want to look hotter by comparison. Now comes' the realization by the ugly one that the other two aren't really her friends, they look at each other, and the tallest prettiest one pulls her purse to her chest, squints her eyes and whispers 'sorry.' I think they shattered the oinkers heart. She's not crying, just blank, she's blankly staring at her *friends* as they walk in. This would be funny if her glare wasn't creeping me out.

"I don't want to see it out of context," Shawn snaps me out of my trance.

"What? Oh, the movie. Come on," I can't let her in. She's still standing to the side quiet, staring at us like we just raped and killed her cat. I can't let her in here. She doesn't belong, she's well below the five-six tossup.

"Nope."

"Hey, I had the weirdest dream last night."

"What happ…"

Jamie swings out, leaning forward, holding onto the doorframe with her left hand, "Hey can one of you come in? We got a nasty ass drunk."

"Really, this early?" thanks for the save Jamie, this hardly happens this early.

"Yeah, you comin' to help?" she asks.

"Yeah I'm comin' babe," she grabs my hand gently.

Shawn looks at me, "Babe?"

"Shawn cover."

"You sure?"

"You had your break, cover. And watch Last Tango!"

"Never gonna happen, babe."

"Shut up,"

Yes, I call her 'Babe', it's a friendly pet name. Jamie is one of the bartenders here; we started working around the same time and just got along from the start. She and I haven't had sex and probably never will. We're in what we call a 'frelationship', literally the complete opposite of friends with benefits: we hang out, go out, talk trash about those around us and occasionally cook dinner for each other. We've cuddled. Stop what you're thinking, it meant nothing. She was breaking up with her ass of a boyfriend, and I said she could crash for a while. We've fallen asleep in each other's arms' watching movies a couple of times. Shut up. I like what we have. I respect her too much to fuck casually, and I like her too much for casual screwing not to turning into something serious. Rule three. But damn she does have a great ass. Best nights of sleep I ever had was with that thing pressed up against my crotch. I wonder what she's doing later.

**Friday, 12:55am, Mind Eraser**

The club is like every other high end night club in the northeast. A dark shadowy place with terrible auto-tuned music that's almost indistinguishable from shitty late nineties techno filled with the grunts and moans of the dancing partisans. The floor is black tile, fake marble, the actual bar is near the door, framed by violet neon lights, three bartenders ten feet apart host it: Jamie is usually the one closest to the door, Ron in the middle, and Dalia at the other end. I don't know Ron well either because he doesn't want to know me or he's just closed off, regardless I tend to keep my distance because he gives me the creeps. Dalia hates both Shawn and I. Shawn because he hit it and quit it, understandably of course, the reason she hates me is well… she thought I was a different breed than Shawn.

In my first week here I took her to my place and gave her my best. I took her out on the town now and again, never defining what we were. She slept over a couple times a week but nothing too extreme for me to call it a relationship. This continued for almost two months then she finally said those horrifying words 'I think I might love you' I flipped my shit and came clean about who I am and my view on relationships. When Dalia found out she was just one of many she was more than a little upset but accepted the role of fuck buddy, then she started questioning my friendship with Jamie. I think she got jealous. I stopped texting her after she yelled 'if you like her so much then why don't you get her to suck your dick'. There are few things that can get me to stop texting instead of letting things run their natural course but yelling at me about my other relationships is number one in my book. She still glares at me when I walk in, even now three or four years after we officially stopped seeing each other she still glares. I don't deny she's still cute and can't say I don't want to sleep with her again but that ship has sailed long ago on both ends. I tend to avoid her as much as I can and she likewise.

DJ cocksucker, the talentless hack who I suspect has been stealing from the tip jar, is in the middle of the arena surrounded by bacchanalian delight. On the left-hand side of the DJ's booth about twenty ought' passes is the bathroom, skank territory where a BJ is almost always guaranteed. Now the bouncer becomes the cooler; have you seen Road House? Well except for the fake drama, overly choreographed fight scenes and me having to liberate a town from the yoke of some spoiled rich guy this is a lot like that. The rules are pretty simple. Try to get a disruptive individual out as peacefully as possible, if they refuse, walk them out, peacefully. Don't use more force than you need to, and always be polite. The good thing about people being drunk is their reflexes, they are significantly slower.

Jamie walks me in, the sound is deafening. I tug on her hand, and she looks back at me.

"What are you doing later?" I yell, she can't hear.

"What?" I can't hear her either I can just read lips. She cups her ear and brings it close.

"Want to watch a movie at my place when we're out?" she smiles, nods yes and gives me a thumbs up then points out the drunk: male, five nine, average build, between age twenty-one and twenty-five, loud, slurred speech, high self-esteem and not as tough as he thinks.

He's yelling at the tenders who refuse to serve him anymore. Dalia's terrified half cowering while still trying to take other orders and Ron is staring at him not saying anything or even reacting. I must be as polite as possible, that is my mantra, be polite. He is far enough away from the speakers so that we can sort of hear each other. I tap his shoulder.

"Hey buddy, let's go."

"One more drink," Or…why thank you kind bouncer I'll be off, and you have a good evening.

"No, now!"

"Leave me alone," strike two.

"Sir, you're not gonna get served, you're embarrassing yourself, and it's just best if you were to leave. So if you will humor me please?"

"Eat shit and die," did you mean 'I never thought of it that way.' No, I'm kidding that's strike three. Time to walk out; putting my arm around the guy's shoulder, he shakes it off. "The fucks the matter with you, queer," I was shot at today, I ain't dealin' with your shit.
Jamie looks at me, I cool down a little. Let's let that one slide and give him a warning.

"Out now before I kick your motherfucking ass," as I say this from the corner of my eye I catch Jamie blowing me a kiss, at least I think it's to me. My heart is pounding, eyes losing focus, something is rotten in Denmark. I think I'm ready for anything he throws at me. Dalia is staring at me, I don't know who she's going root for.

He threw the first punch, honest. I only blinked and shit got crazy, the music stopped, and I was in the middle of a circle of people. What I knew and what I saw were worlds apart; he threw the first punch, that I know, but his nose and mouth are gushing blood, and I'm pretty sure those are his teeth spread out on the ground alongside shattered glass. I check my teeth to make sure, all there. He's a bloody mess. The lights are dimming I can't see much through the shadows except the pool of blood growing around his figure. Some chick behind me starts screaming 'murderer' pointing at me. As the lights brighten I see Jamie's face is long and white, contorted into a horrible twisted expression that I can't fully describe nor can I get out of my head, she's shaking. As the lights dim again her eyes still linger in the shadows filled with horror. Ron is washing blood off the counter pretending that he doesn't see me while a smirk grows under his brow. I knew he had a screw loose. Did he attack this guy? Dalia is screaming her head off, she's creeping behind Ron putting her back against the wall hiding from me. A few guys start clapping. I look into the mirror and see two people in the back somewhere break out fighting.

I am the center of the universe, all eyes fall on me. Aw, applause, and condemnation. I have lived under the radar for so long and now suddenly I'm a fucking beacon calling out to everyone around. I am Jack hear me roar. All I can think is 'what the hell happed' over and over again with the image of Jamie's terrified face flashing from the shadows, did he knock himself out? How can I shut this annoying bitch up? Why is no one stopping those guys from fighting? Pressure is building, my head is about to blow. There's acid flowing through my veins and needles in my eyes. A shearing blade is running deep in my mind, slow and dull, it's cutting into every nerve, and now all thought is blank. Is this the end for Jack Fabbrico? Tune in next week for the startling conclusion.

# Part II

Diary of the Other Guy

And we're back...

**Friday, 3:23 am, A Bird in the Hand, a Bird in the Cage**

As my brain reboots, I think back at the string of flash memories that I have. From my recollections I went through the usual jailhouse preceding: printing, information, evaluation of my risk, looking back at my priors, and obviously the phone. They're just tryin' to roll up my bill. I don't think I talked to a counselor but what do I know? It's pretty late, and I'm pretty out of it. I'm losing it, I feel as though I'm in a new room every time I open my eyes. Now I'm stuck in the tank; sometimes in great turmoil I become a shell, not exactly catatonic but frozen, I need to recoup my mindset, and the only thing I think I can move are my eyes. I scroll over the entirety of the cell. There are eight bars running vertical in the door, four running horizontal, there are seven other guys held in here and a crack going from my feet to the door. The walls are a void, light gray vacant of all expression. The floors have small discolored spots all around from decades of chewing gum, spit, shit and jiz that have been stomped into the concrete. There are five wooden benches, three that outline the walls of the cage and the others two run parallel to the one on the back wall. I'm on the bench closest to the door.

Those locked in here with me are keeping their distance. Apparently what scares fat ass bikers, neo-Nazis and gang bangers (I think one of the two hoodlums in here is that gun crazed Chicano from earlier or maybe wife beaters and do-rags are just what the kids today are wearing, you know the shit bag craze) is one man dressed all in black not moving, not talking, covered in blood. If I look at them, I can see a shiver run up their spines. I fucked up big time, please kill me. Hours have passed, I need help. I go deep into my memories and drown out the world.

I think of Halloween in sixth grade where I dressed as the Norse God Loki, I bleached my hair and dyed it red. I went to a party with Hannah and Rachel, no one knew who I was supposed to be. My mind wanders to the first time I went paddle boarding and convinced Anne to try it. She fell off and gashed her leg open, she never went to the beach again after that. I think forward a little to when sister Sullivan bent over picking up her rosaries, and I did the 'accidental' bump and squeeze. Father Ferrara saw what I did laughed then took me aside after the fleeting of the congregation to chastise me. That was the last time I went to services, the hypocrisy just got to me. I mean he saw, he laughed and he probably would've done the same thing in my shoes but chose to chew me out for the hell of it. My mind continues with a series of short vignettes; essentially it starts out as a collage of titty porn, then the girls become more familiar, they become the girls of my past and present dressed in skin tight black leather holding whips, paddles, cat o'nine-tail and other malicious toys. I best stop thinking these thoughts. Jail isn't the best place to have a boner. No cold shower in sight, I do what all boys do when they want to stop an erection, I think of mom.

"This is not normal John, you are wrong, wrong!" she screams at me.

"I'm not wrong. Mom, you need help," I say in a cold manner.

My mother had been admitted to this assisted living for around a year by this time, some place that was sympathetic to our situation. I think dad may have flipped the bill. I came to visit one day with Anne, she was most human when dealing with our mother. I notice her hair was quickly turning grey and she had lost control of the muscles in her face causing frequent ticks and a downward slant on the left side of her mouth. Her eyes were so tired that day; black and sad and pained. This is the last time I paid my mother a visit when she could walk. She tried to claw me with her boney fingers, luckily loons aren't entitled to fingernails.

"Why are you doing this to me?" she begs for freedom.

"I'm not doing anything," I pull my arm away.

Anne grabs mom's hand gently, petting it, "you're here to be helped," a concerned smile is the only one in her repertoire.

"Who are you? Another one of Dan's whores, right?" she rips her hand away, disgusted.

"Mom that's Anne."

"I knew he named my baby after one of his girls, let go of me," dad was a player? Weird.

Mom slapped Anne across the face, and I couldn't hold back my laughter. A few nurses and orderlies rushed in, jumping on her. They knocked her out and brought her back to her room. Anne and I never spoke of that day again. I don't know if seeing my family at its lowest point is better or worse than being locked up, I saw my mom go crazy, but I also saw Anne get bitch slapped. It's a tradeoff.

      The door rattles, I stand and step forward, "Fabbrico, Johnathan," a familiar voice called, almost immediately I am brought to the courthouse and thrown in front of a judge with a pink curler dangling from her hair. The arraignment has begun. This never happens.

      "Does the defendant wish to waive the reading of the charges?" she asks.

      "No," she sighs.

      "Very well," she licks her lips and pulls up my file, adjusting her glasses she begins "Fabbrico, Johnathan: you are being tried on one account of assault and battery at one twelve a.m. to one Fredrich Klaus, disrupting the peace and causing property damage to your employer Mr. Angelus. Do you understand the charges being presented before you today?"

      The clerk standing at my side, a skinny kid, looks nervous, his tie is too big and he hasn't a jacket. I can see in his anxious movements he plans on pleading not guilty once the judge looks his way. He looks at me to answer her.

      "I do," so… are we married? She looks over to my clerk, I raise my cuffed hands over his mouth. The bailiff takes a step towards me gripping his club and my clerk flinches, the judge motions her hands settling everyone down knowing that my action meant 'I disagree with my counsel.'

      "Have you plans to hire or accept any form of counsel?"

      "No your honor, I will be defending myself today."

      "Interesting," she avoids eye contact thinking I'll make a fool of myself. "How do you plead?"

Not guilty, I would be an idiot if I said otherwise, right?

      "I'd like to request a motion for dismissal," her head jolts up, I have her full attention.

      "A bit early, we have only just begun."

      "Well, early bird gets the worm."

      "And which are you, the bird or the worm?"

I say nothing.

"Have you evidence or a defensive argument to support your motion?"

"Though I will admit to my actions they must be excused on the grounds of self-defense and the protection of the greater good, i.e. the other customers and employees."

"May I ask how you have come to this conclusion?"

"Well… your honor, he did attempt to throw a punch at me," she interrupts me with a hum of affirmation, "also, do to my profession and all that it entails, the use of force is a necessity if the situation calls for it. My job is to protect the peace of my employers' establishment, is it not?" again she hums 'yeah'. "So with that comes the safety of the customers and in the instance of a belligerent individual with impaired mental faculties, a drunk who lacked control over his or her actions, did create a dangerous environment that required an amount of force that may have appeared excessive from an outside perspective to ensure the safety of those around," she looks a little surprised at my pleading. She clears her throat, my clerk and the prosecutor walk up to the bar and they converse. While they decide my fate I spaced out thinking about mom, thinking maybe temporary insanity would have been better, just waiting for a number set for bail. Then I looked at the magistrate as they disperse and tuned back into the program.

"After reviewing all the evidence, the opinions of the defense and prosecution, and giving the nature of your occupation along with your pleading. There appears to have been some extenduating circumstances that demonstrate that you were," the judge pauses, bites her lip, looks down, then at me, then at Rachel, yes Rachel, "within your legal right to use force if need be to ensure peace, you are hereby acquitted of all charges," she drops the gavel on the podium opposed to striking, stands, doesn't look at me and leaves the room. The bailiff comes to unlock my cuffs. I turn around with a huge smile looking at the helpful minx that got me off. Rachel, on the other hand, does not appear so enthused.

Now here is where things get bad. I called Rachel to see if she would bail me out. I didn't call because she's a cop, ok maybe a little of that too, but mainly because she was the only person who I knew would answer my call. Siobhan, my little

Joani, refused to help me. She was the first person I called, I thought she might be a little sympathetic to my predicament or maybe just want to make it up to me after this evening but no. She said this isn't her problem and I should sort it out myself then gave me the number of a lawyer and told me not to mention her name. Two fucking years, quite literally years of just fucking around and I thought we were *friends*. I know my sister won't bail me out again, Michelle is still paranoid.

There's Vanessa and Samantha, but their significant others would hate their leaving at this hour, I would have called Shawn, but he's not at his place tonight. Jamie, oh Jamie, I wouldn't want her to see me like this. The one call policy is true, sort of, you can get another one but usually there's a large fee that follows after bail, and it really depends on if the guard is in the mood to be of assistance. I had to bribe the jailor with my watch and fifty bucks just to get a second call. The good news is my watch is only worth like fifteen bucks so fuck him.

What I'm getting at is having a long list of names doesn't guarantee help when it's needed; these are first and foremost shallow relationships, nothing is expected on either end so don't think bad of my people. Rachel came to my rescue. A person I hadn't seen in forever cares more about me than anyone else in the world. Well, that's what I thought anyway when she mumbled 'I'll take care of it, sit tight' in that half dozed tone. I just wanted out. I didn't expect her to organize an appearance immediately after I called, let alone get me off all charges.

We're walking down the hall surrounded by cops and lawyers that avoid making eye contact with either of us. She's quiet, eyes focused on getting out of here without being seen. She consistently holds a stern look as she marches down these halls, she's three steps in front of me at all times. A storm's a comin'. I move faster, she moves faster. Her head is fixed forward, I can't see those beautiful ogles. At least the door is coming close. Exiting, I know not what fresh hell I'm about to endure on the outside of these walls, but I will accept it when she tears into me.

"You are a fucking idiot! You know that right?"

"I think that's a matter of opinion."

"Don't be cute. Do you know the shit storm you got me in?" she pokes me in the chest, her slender pointer is still at me as I step back and look at her hand, her ring finger is sans-band.

"I'm sorry."

"You're sorry. Do you know how much you cost me? Do you?" I take a deep breath in.

"A favor you wanted to tuck away for a rainy day, possibly a stain on your badge as a new cop in this department and or up to five thousand dollars in bail. But seeing as no court date was set and the judge did say 'excused' or better yet 'acquitted' if memory serves it reads, to me at least, that there was no bail. I am a free man. Now that's not usually how an arraignment works, is it? I mean a case can be thrown out but not during the first meet up. So tell me. What did you do?" She's silent.

"Come on, smile," I pat her shoulder, "I'll get you a cup of coffee, and I'll tell you what happened."

"You're unbelievable," is that a bad thing? "I know what happened."

"Then hear my side and tell me what they're saying, just one cup. That's all I'm asking."

"Why are you pushing this?"

"Because I'm tired and owe you at least a cup of coffee."

"A cup of coffee?" standing under the light posts, favoring her left side. She is glimmering, just the reflection of beauty; her hair messy, skin glowing and eyes so bright and so soft. Even with her arms crossed and super pissed at me I can't help but be happy that she's back in my life. I think she just forgave me.

"Ok, several thousand cups and a few biscotti."

"How about a muffin too?" she's looking down all innocent like, trying to suppress a smile as she steps closer to me.

"What am I, made of money?" I got her to laugh, well I freed that smile. I don't know how much it cost her, she refused to say, she didn't mention money really or a favor, maybe her badge alone got me out.

**Friday, 6:10 am Served...**

I'm not speaking, I haven't said a word since we got in her car and she remains quiet as well. The only sounds come from the engine, a creaking from her suspension as we hit bumps and potholes, and the A/C. We have just entered Fall River. Yet again Troy has fallen. This dilapidated hole is my home away from home. From the mad-dog personality you may see, this city is essentially what the bastard offspring of Boston raping Brooklyn would be like; angry, scared and in some sick way beautiful. I've been in a lot of cities, bad areas, at night and I will admit I have felt a sense unease. Usually when walking down an ally or rundown boroughs alone and I hear the footsteps of someone behind me gaining traction, gaining speed. In those situations I think I might get robbed or shot, but here, at night, it's different. I've always felt that this city is an entity of corruption, something that rots its citizens from the inside out; in this city I often imagen that at any moment someone might come up, drug, rob, shoot, and rape me, in that order. See what I mean by beautiful. Despite it scaring the hell out of me, and nothing bad actually ever happening, I still like to come here once in a while for the food and the people. But mostly the food.

History lesson. Before it was Troy, before it was anything this pulsating gothic shadow was divided between Freetown, known mainly for the winning battle three years in the Revolutionary war, and Tiverton, meaning the settlement that would become Fall River was broken between Mass and little Rhody which explains the conflicted feelings you have when stepping foot on the grounds. This city, when it became a city, was founded on the production and shipping of textiles. Being on the water, it was easy for mills to set up shop and start spinning thread, making it at one point economically prosperous though it is hard to see anything that resembles prosperity today. You might not know much about this city, or anything for that matter, but there is one lovely little lady that you may have heard of, someone whose family made this city what it was and what it is today, Lizzie Andrew Borden.

Lizzie Borden whose name lives on in the hearts of every child here through the nursery rhyme '*Lizzie Borden took an axe and gave her mother forty whacks, when she saw what she had done she gave her father forty-one.'* On August forth 1892 she had killed her stepmother Abby with twenty or so hits to the head with a hatchet, Andrew, her father was struck eleven times while he slept. His eye was cut clean in half. When she was questioned during the investigation she would often give different accounts of what happened that day, a red flag if you ask me. June fifth, 1893 a trial began in New Bedford for the ax-wielding maniac. Primarily because she lacked a dick and was considered emotionally incapable of the act she, on June twentieth, was acquitted of all charges. The system has hardly changed since then I suppose. Why I mention this I don't know, I guess only psychos understand psychos.

I start reflecting on the night. What had I done? I can't get rid of that image of everyone in the club terrified, surrounding me. The pain creeps back in my head, a pulsing arises from behind my left eye. I imagine Jamie in the back seat still carrying that look of horror; those condemning eyes, her pupils shrinking so to not let light through, casting me into an eternal shadow. She's staring right through me. Calling me a monster. Those floating eyes as I see them now shine fowl in the rear view.

"What the hell is wrong with you? I was doing my job God damn it," I thought at the ghost.

"Well…" my imagined specter begins.

"Let's get a pick-me-up," Rachel interrupted my delusion, breaking the awkward silence while pulling over.

We stopped to talk and have a cup o' Joe in a café down deep in the heart of Fall River on the way home, she knew the area well. Once we took a seat, she continued trying to pull me out of my mood. Rachel, without being asked began telling me her life story, from Carolina all the way back here. Her college days, she attended East Carolina U and dropped out the begging of her junior year, she wanted to be a vet but didn't have the grades. She decided to be a cop on a coin toss, it was either police academy or the military, she wanted to get as far away from her fam as possible and basically ran away as soon as she raised enough money for a ticket north. Rachel told me that at one point circling back to her roots she waitressed here, spending late nights paying for her training and supporting herself. She met Maxi in this lil'establishment. It's a cool looking place; retro fifty-sixties style, the walls are black with a silver plated frame just below the windows and just before the floor. The stools and counter are black-and-white, the booths are marron and quite soft. The tv spewing out KENO numbers rests on top of the desert fridge, it looks and feels a lot like Anne's place but with a soul, of course. We're the only people here other than the staff. A busboy is sweeping up the floor from the rush that let loose a few hours earlier.

I'm disgusted with our waitress. She's old; sixties, seventies. Her eyes are sad and broken down. Her uniform consists of a bright yellow shirt and sweatpants. She moves slow. Her cheeks hang low, and she has a neck wattle. She looks like a sick basset hound in constant fear that her owner is about to put her down if she piddles on the floor again. I only looked at her for a few seconds, that's all I needed to memorize her face. I decide to keep my eyes on Rachel and try to forget about the waitress. Stuck in my head, the volume is lowering. Her words play as whispers.

I can't believe how good she still looks after all this time, her training kept her body tight. I'm smiling as the pain of her absent years builds, so close yet so far away and without even a phone call. Eventually, I will explode saying 'what happened' or 'did you ever think about me,' so she doesn't think I don't care or my life is a total waste. I'm not even really listening to what she's saying at this point except when I hear the name 'Max' and the sour taste of copper comes up in the back of my throat. The bile is building in my stomach, I can feel the black sludge churning as I sip on my cup of coffee, an ulcer is forming in my gullet. I hate everything right now.

She continues and I twitch and suffer, my legs rapidly jolt up and down as a twinge in my groin grows intense makes her company intolerable, I can't take it anymore it feels like someone is jamming a piano wire up my urethra. I can keep the screaming in my head, that is until I inevitably blurt out.

"I didn't hit him," I think I may have just yelled that in a public place.

"What?"

"I mean I don't know, I don't remember hitting him and even if I did he threw the first punch. Self-defense."

"Whoa, where did that come from?"

"I just want to put it on record that I did not hit him. That is my official statement."

"Since *now*... it doesn't matter you don't need to have an official statement," then she leans-in to whisper "and Jack I saw the tapes."

"Then you know," she sits back and starts stirring sugar in her coffee.

"That you're lying to me, yeah!" her eyes are bugging out of her head. You're cute when you're angry.

"I'm not lying, I know exactly what happened I asked him to leave, he wouldn't he just... he became belligerent, started arguing with me as I was trying to get him to leave. Then he threw a punch, I blinked, and I don't know, the next thing I saw was him on the floor."

"That makes no sense," actually it makes *almost* no sense, you forget I'm crazy.

"It's what happened."

"So the evidence is wrong? All of it?"

"Yes."

"The testimonies of everyone Julia K. Nimbse, Samson Rockford, Charles Xavier."

Did she just say Charles Xavier?

"Did you just say Charles Xavier?"

"Yeah?"

"I'm being judged by the X-men?"

"Yeah, I guess," she's looking down at her coffee.

"I guess all hope is gone now."

"What are you saying?" she's lost.

"You never got into comics, did you?"

"No," figures. Well perfection is an idea, not a reality.

"Anyway... all the people in there were drinking, they can't give an accurate statement. Any lawyer would argue that."

"There's so much about the law you don't know?" she's almost laughing.

"Did they question anyone sober?"

"Your employer: João Angelus. In the file, he said that he saw you 'going berserk' his words and gave us access to the clubs DVR."

Ah João, João, João. João Angelus is how you would imagine a grease ball personified by the mythical Pan, he has the libido of the ram and the appeal of a shit stain. He is roughly five foot two and balding, he always wears sunglasses which seem to constantly be sliding down his enormous nose, he is stalky without being fat, holding all his weight on his arms and chest. João is the proud owner of the third hippest joint in Providence, which would be a greater feat if he didn't have others on his black-out payroll infest his competitors with rats and roaches. His philosophy is almost Hobbesian, mans' natural state is war. Angelus says if you want to win you can't be afraid to kill those with a leg up in this world. He's not only physically repugnant, but his beliefs are utterly offensive. João is one of the most racist people I have come across; I don't know how the hell Shawn got hired or how he had enough leverage to get me a job. Essentially João hates just about everyone who isn't English, Irish or Portuguese.

Sleaze just spews out of him, so much so that he can't be on the floor of his own establishment during operating hours for two reasons. One he doesn't meet his own qualifications for what you're supposed to look like and two he can't control himself around the women. Between you, me and the deep blue sea, he's had to buy the silence of a few girls in his day. I hate him more than anyone I have ever met, and the feeling is mutual. I once spit a shot of Patron in his eyes after he slapped Jamie's ass right in front of me as she bent down to unplug the neon-lights over the bar. Thus starting our 'you no fuck with me I no fuck with you' truce, or de taunt as I call it. I keep my job, and his staff won't bleed him dry in lawsuits. Apparently, I have or had that much pull with the staff. João has no honor, no rules, and no class. He is ignorant on all accounts. The very sight of him makes me sick.

"He has it in for me."

"Oh? What's his motive?"

"Maybe I come in a little late, maybe slept with his mistress or I steal a bottle now and again. I can't pinpoint the exact reason."

"What?"

"What? He pays me shit, and I deserve something nice now and again."

"No, the mistress thing."

Yeah... I may have left that tidbit out. Well, I said I hated him, I never said anything about his women. Granted it started out as hate fucking but she was too gorgeous for me to take my aggression out on: long black hair, pale skin, trim, draped all in black. Like Elvira crossed with Lauren Bacall, sexy and mysterious and funny. She used to come round the club at the end of pre-shift, linger around the bar nursing drinks for a few hours or be in the office for most of the night if not all of it, and then leave with the rest of us at closing. I flirted with her when I first started learning how to mix drinks, she was my test subject. I quickly discovered that she was incredibly bright, I could talk to her for hours on end on any subject, and she could keep pace. But that was before the agreement of João and I, otherwise we would have kept in touch.

"Oh, well I wouldn't sleep with his wife, he won't even do that."

"What the hell happened to you?"

Let's see: I was madly in love with you, you never looked me over, you moved without telling me which left a hollow feeling of abandonment ingrained in my every waking moment that I try to fill with nonstop bouts of unavailable women. You know, the usual soul-crushing reasons.

"I don't know what you're talking about," I'm a fucking idiot!

"You were such a nice kid," excluding that limerick preventing you from getting a date, I guess I was alright.

"Nah, I've always been rude, crude and a bit lewd," she touches my hand gently.

"That's not how I remember you," a smile! What's on your mind?

"How do you remember me then?" am I really fishing for a compliment from the woman who just got me out of jail? I touch her hand back, and we lock fingers. Yes, yes I am.

"I remember you, Jack, as a quiet, sensitive, albeit distant boy who had his nose in a comic book half the time and under girls skirt the rest, but would always be there for me whenever I needed him. Not this."

"And what, pray tell, is this?" go ahead, rip me a new one.

"A violent degenerate attacking civilians with tequila bottles."

"Wait, what?"

"Security cameras, Jack. I saw everything you did. Kinda hard to falsify video in that short period of time."

"I didn't do that. I swear! Cross my heart and hope to die. Come on, why would I lie to you?"

"I don't know why, but I saw them, the guy fell trying to hit you then you beat the living shit out of him, hopped behind the bar grabbed a bottle, pushed that short girl out of the way," she must mean Dalia, "and... and... God damn it, you bashed his head open," she pulls her hand away and covers her mouth. "I can never un-see that. What the fuck?" she snapped out of that short break of nostalgia and remembers what just happened, please don't look at me like that Rachel.

"I didn't do that," I love you.

"You keep saying that but I just can't believe you, I know what I saw."

"You have to believe me. Rachel, please," me grasping at the coat of a woman about to leave, what is this world coming to?

"I don't have to do anything, I've done my part. Good bye Johnny boy," she tugs on her coat breaking my grip.

"What? Rachel! Please..." she walks out.

So that's it, the one woman whose opinion I really cared about doesn't even want to hear what I have to say. She had no interest in me after all. This was just a pity date, coffee, whatever. Rachelle wanted me out of her life and wanted me to know it. This isn't the first time I was told 'I can't see you anymore' and it won't be the last. I bury myself in every sad love story I've read or seen, comparing myself to every man who lost their girl. *Tu oublieras aussi Henriette*, a pen and napkin are poor substitutes for a diamond and window. 'Here's to looking at you, kid' damn it Bogey. I'm a cold bastard but I can't deal with losing Rachel like this, I don't want whatever good memories she may have of me to die. It's probably easier to say bye if you go out looking like a hero, at least you can say you did the right thing and know that's how you'll be remembered.

"Ok, you have five," I have been wrong before, "I'm not saying I believe you, I'm not saying I don't. Honestly, I don't know what I'm saying. I just think there's more here and I can't know it without hearing everything."

"You're back," I did not see that coming.

"Yeah, don't make a big deal out of it and hurry I'm tired as shit, and you have one chance not to make me walk out that door, now go."

"Ok, where do I start?"

"The beginning."

"I was born on a Sunday night, my mom was screaming, and blood was everywhere, and…"

"I'm out of here," she slams her hands on the counter and begins to stand.

"No, wait. Start where? That day, the hour, the minute; where do you want me to start?"

"When you got to work up till the incident."

"I punched in," wrong vocabulary, "around nine-twenty, nine-thirty. I was working with Shawn, we let those in who looked good and those who didn't we bounced, a few hours in Shawn screwed some girl in the back alley. Once he got back, Jamie called me in to eject a particularly troublesome individual."

"I take it that was the guy."

"That it was, Raunchy. That it was."

"So then what happened?" she's eager, leaning in close to me. I love this.

"I don't really know, I mean I know what I saw and what happened, but it doesn't make much sense to me now."

"What?"

"If you stop interrupting I'll tell you, et hem…he threw a punch at me, I blinked, I saw two people fighting in the background then there was blood everywhere, no I saw the blood then I saw the people fighting," I close my eyes trying to focus and imagine the evening. "No, I don't know. Everyone is staring at me," the pressure builds again, I can't think. Suddenly I'm struck with hot flashes and stills of the night filled with gore and blood and anger and panic. I see bits of glass imbedded in macerated pulped flesh, long strands of blood stretching like webs stuck to the floor. I see all this accompanied with the annoying oomph of the music pounding in my ear, "I just want it to stop. But no one else looked at the fighters in the back. Everyone just staring at me," my head is pounding. I look down rubbing my eyes, "I just want them all to stop looking at me, please," it hurts so much.

"What do you mean background?" she touches my elbow and I look up. Her beautiful face, the pain is gone.

"The back, a ways away from the bar on the dance floor. I saw them in the mirror."

"No one else noticed two people fighting?"

"No," I'm sick of this game.

"Let me ask you this, were you on any drugs?"

"Caffeine."

"So no drugs, do you remember going to jail?"

"Sort of."

"'Sort of'? How do you not remember being taken to jail?"

"I remember handcuffs, being put in a cell, printed and someone asking me questions or something. I don't know," my head, not this again. Can someone dim the lights? Or just kill me, I'm good with either.

"Specifics, do you remember that specifically?"

"I don't know!" he yelled trying to get through to the woman he loved.

"Are you remembering and know that's what happened or do you just think you remember?"

"No."

"No to what?" her voice echoes louder and louder.

"Just no. I don't remember."

"I know a little psych," don't all women? "Do you know what a fugue state is?" what is a disordered state of mind in which somebody typically wanders or does an action without recollection of said action, Trebek?

"No, I've never heard of that," liar!

"Basically you can have gaps in your memory and can still be doing something, sometimes there are hallucinations. In severe cases, it can be like multiple personality disorder," don't you mean dissociative identity disorder? Don't want to offend the loonies.

"You think that happened to me?"

"It's the only explanation to how you could have sodomized a guy with a bottle and not done it at the same time," wait, what the fuck?

"What the fuck did I actually do with the bottle?" I'm thrown into a small panic: looking around the restaurant, twitching, I scratch my cheek, discreetly trying to smell my hand.

"You didn't sodomize anyone," she breaks out laughing. "I was just seeing if you were legit."

"What?"

"Don't worry you checked out," first time you checked me out.

"I see," says the blind man to the deaf mute, "thank you," I calm down.

"Not a problem, it's kind of hard for me to see you as a bad guy," she relaxes into the booth, stretching her arm ontop of the backrest.

"Well, I'm not a good guy either."

"That's hard to believe."

"How? I sleep around, mess with people, fuck with their heads, their lives, and my job is superficiality incarnate. Sweetie, I ain't good."

"I've known you longer, and I probably shouldn't say anything," she leans her head back, yawns, and looks behind her for a sec before returning to the conversation, hunching over the table, on her elbows, "but I did think you were kind of cute when we were kids," she quickly seals her lips and looks away.

"You fancy me," I say quickly in a proud, nasally exagerated Boston accent. She rappidly turns her head back to me.

"I did when you weren't this."

"When I wasn't this I was kind of a... loser, I never got what I wanted."

"And what did you want?"

"Well, back then I guess mmm..." I don't know how to write muddled gibberish. Sorry.

"What was that?" when a girl smiles like this with wide eyes, leaning forward, their hands folded over each other, you can tell they know exactly what you said they just want to screw with you a little and sometimes it's fun to play their games.

"You. I hads' the hots fors ya back in the day."

"Why didn't you say anything?" because you never seemed like you liked me. she leans back twirling her curls.

"I don't know. Why didn't you?" prepare for incoming bullshit.

"Your sister sort of told me not to mess with you, account of coach Souza," damn it, Anne, fucking with my sex life even back then. "And that weird limerick that came about," not touching that one, I finally got her to smile again. Oh, I have to tell her about the coach.

"Hey, Rachel..."

"Oh, yeah I forgot to tell you. This may sound weird but do you remember Souza?"

"Yeah actually I..."

"Shhh... I don't want you to be too surprised," oh no. "I actually," is this actually happening? "married coach Souza, Max. I kept my last name," that's it. My life is over. She married a guy who's like thirty years older than her. Ew...

"He's like thirty years older than you."

"Only twenty-two."

"Why... how... why!"

"He strolled into this place about four years ago, I waitressed, and he was just so sad," you think?

"So? Pity fuck him and move on like a normal person."

"I ruined his life."

"Pity fuck and a free cup of coffee! Something a little less permanent."

"Why are you getting so defensive?" not only are you fucking a man about twice your age, you're not fucking me.

"I don't know, you married a guy for the wrong reasons."

"What's wrong with being with a man who supports me, would do anything to make me feel comfortable and is very forgiving," is he good in the sack?

"It's out of desperation," also he's so fucking old.

"We support each other."

"Do you love him?"

Blank stare, "...Of course, I do," kind of slow with the response, this is the many kinds of love story. "I mean I'm not saying we never fight or anything, but he's really sweet."

"Sweet... sweet... hmmm."

"What?"

"I asked if you love him."

"And I said of course."

"True, but you had to defend it. You felt it necessary to explain. Love is irrational by nature, it need not be explained. You, my dear officer of truth and justice, are a liar."

"Hey, I love him."

"Like a father I'm sure," I stand and throw down a few dollars, "well it's late, or early, whatever. Anyway, I should call a cab. Electra nice to meet you and uh... enjoy killing your mother," leaving her now would be leaving who I was and getting over my past and I really, really, should do that right now before my life gets any more convoluted. Remember rule three about emotions and having to always move on, it's for this exact reason.

"Hey... Jack come back here for a minute, sit, sit down," I stop in front of the door, I look to see her waving me back. What? I said I should leave; I don't necessarily have to, hey they're my rules.

"What?"

"I heard you out. You should hear what I have to say."

"Ok, but I have something to say first."

I am Diogenes...

**Friday, 5:30pm, Secrets**
*Si una donna e tranquila, ha bisogno un uomo.*
Translation: if a woman is at peace then she needs a man. The subtext in there is 'to ruin it.' Ok, I know, I'm a douche for not sharing the art of persuasion, as I know it, with you but I couldn't be sure if it would work. Yet, I feel if you've been paying attention at all you could piece together what happened. Looky here, she's still asleep. I mean I had to shift some things in my schedule around, Terri and Melony, but I got the Raunch. I caught the Raunch. I caught... the Raunch. I still can't fucking believe it, I caught the Raunch! I'm so giddy. Look at her; that ginger hair all in disarray brushing over her sweet shoulders. She's lying on her stomach, her face turned towards me, mouth closed showing off those soft lips, and the light smattering of freckles that cross the bridge of that button nose.

She went down like scotch. First like an Islay, I felt the heat of that amber colored minx and like her liquor counterpart she came strong. Then after an hour she became like a Speyside, got sweeter, and took me down by the third or fourth bout, and I gave up all control. I am hers. My shoulder looks like a chew toy and my wrists still show the indents left by her cuffs. Though she may look angelic there's some demon in there, I tend to bring that out in people. I don't know if that's good or bad.

She rolls over, and now I can fully appreciate those curves mhmmm... I slide the tip of my finger slowly and gently from the point of her chin down her neck, between those marvelous breasts and to her naval. Her skin is velvet. Come here look, the age old question, I lift the sheet, does the carpet match the drapes? Answer: inconclusive, waxing ouchy. Wow, what do you think C's? D's? Yes, I'm a pig but what's the point in always watching your mouth. That just makes you into a liar. I gotta get a drink of water, she kinda squeezed me dry. Yeah, yeah I brought her to my place after I have implied that to be a big no-no, but let me ask you this: where the hell would you bring her? A motel, a hotel? No, she's far too special for that. Come with me to the kitchen. I really wish I had cleaned this place up though, I should have at least done some dishes when I had the chance. I grab a glass and fill it from the spout.

"Well… well… well…" damn it Jamie, my mind is running wild.

"Why are you here?"

"Why do you want me here?"

"Cus'… I finally slept with Rachel, and I need to tell someone?"

"No, I think that's the point of the diary," she sits in my chair. "Talking to an imaginary friend is an exorcize in problem solving, or a cry for help. Or you're just goin' batshit."

"Then why don't you tell me what I need help with?" I take the love seat.

"Are we going to play this game?" I, grinning stupidly, nod yes, "You're not crazy. I don't know why you like to act like it. Just say what you feel you need someone to hear."

"Then you'll go?"

"I can vanish now if you really want, but I guess you want me here for a reason so spill it mister."

"Ok," I take a deep breath and reflect on the thorn in my paw. "Did I do good?"

"Yes… and no."

"Yes, because I slept with the girl of my dreams? No, because I had to nearly killed a guy to do it?"

"Wrong."

"What then?"

"I know this is a thinking exercise, but you're being incredibly thick, you know it, just say it."

"I'm doing good because I actually care about Rachel."

"Yes. Go on."

"And I'm finally acting like a real person instead of a Looney-Tune with a hard on."

"Yeah. Excluding my presence, I would say so."

"Then tell me, what I did wrong?"

"Let me ask this," she leans forward, elbowing her thigh and rests her chin on her fist. "Why have you never tried to sleep with me?"

"Well, currently you're a figment of my imagination. My hands are free if you want, I just don't think I have enough fluids to spare currently," I hold up my glass. "But give me five, and we'll see where I'm at," I drink.

"Don't play around, why haven't you?"

"Because I respect you too much," I say in a clam, dignified tone.

"And you don't respect Rachel?" I knew this was coming, why do I feel like my balls just dropped?

"I do," I cross my legs, bring my glass close, sheilding my face.

"But not in the same way, right?" she sits up, her face looks bored and angry, and a little offended.

"I wouldn't say that. Respect is not an easy thing to compare," I stall, chewing the rim of my glass, looking away then back, "I met you at work, so maybe there's a little professionalism, I guess. I mean, I met her as a kid, in school. I grew up at her side. Those are completely different environments. I would say that I respect her as much as I respect you. Can't it be that I just don't want to sleep with you?"

"Why not? You fuck everything else that touches you. Why not me, I look a lot like her?"

"Don't flatter yourself sweetheart," I lean back in the chair, spread my legs and drink the rest of my water.

"Maybe not now cus' you don't want to see me like that, but you have to admit there are similarities," she leans forward, "vast similarities," I have a thing for theatrics.

"You're similar heights," I look at my glass and swirl my figure around the rim.

"Ooh yeah huge similarity, deeper you schmuck-wad."

"And both have curly hair."

"So do half the girls you bang, go on."

"Ok..."

"Come on you're not even trying: we're both gingers, similar bust, same cheek structure, same age. Hell, the Batcave's computer wouldn't be able to tell our voices apart!"

"Shhhh... keep your voice down."

"John, you're the only one that can hear me."

"I know it's just getting a little loud in here. You're gonna give me a headache."

"Anyway, you know the only reason you like having me around is that I remind you of her," she crosses her arms, "silly jokes that you feign are off the top of your head you've said a

thousand times to her. We've cuddle, nobody just cuddles a
friend. You invite me over for Easter dinner every year.
Whenever we go to the movies, sitting there, in the dark, your
hand caressing my knee, you're just pretending like she's still
around. Acting like she never left. An age-old obsession John;
you fantasize advice not from Shawn, or your sister, or even
your Joani, but from me. I've never done anything for you. In
fact, it appears that I might even use you at times."

"That not true."

"John they're your memories."

I have nothing to say.

"We're in a frelationship: *I* have a place to crash
whenever *I* want, have someone to gossip to, a date to a friend's
weddings whenever *I*'m single, a home cooked meal if *I* don't
feel like doing anything."

"She cooks for me too."

"Once and it was horrible. How does one time compare
with, I don't know how many?"

"Ok, ok, your point?"

"It can't just be because you hold us both in such high
regard. Why haven't you?"

"Because I'll hurt you!"

"You won't touch me because you fear you'll cheat?
Hell, I've know you long enough to expect you to have a few
playmates, that can't be it," I look away. "You're afraid of me,
of her."

"Why wouldn't I be? I just ran into her today."

"Yesterday."

"Whatever. And within twenty-four hours I nearly killed
a guy, got jealous over an old man and rearranged my entire
fucking schedule."

"Your schedule is very important to you."

"Thank you Captain Obvious. What are you going to say
next? It's a way of distancing myself from emotional situations,
and-and it prevents me from getting too attached? A means of
avoiding my feelings?"

"No, you've said that enough times. You write it down
almost every other page," it's a very important rule.

"Yeah, rule number three."

"But you want a life with her?"

"Duh."

"And you do love her, right? You love her?"

"Stop stating the obvious?"

"Kind of what I do. Well, this therapy sesh is almost over, you wanted me here to resolve this qualm. Forget about the rules, there is no rule three in a real relationship. See what it's like being with someone; whether it's her, or me, or another one of your toys, just try it for a while. I know that's what you want to hear."

"Kay," I turn my head away from her again, biting the tip of my thumb. Chipping away at the nail and skin until I reach nailbed.

"Keep in mind there are two types of people that one loves: the first we love so passionately we would gladly allow them the opportunity to hurt us, we'd even hurt ourselves just to be with them for an hour, and we can never truly trust because of the power they have over us. The other which is a passive love, it burns slow and is often paved with compromise. We find it to be comfortable, that's why we tend to stay with them."

"So which is she?"

"If you don't know chances are I don't."

"Is that it?"

"I guess, but may I leave you with one more thought?"

"Sure."

"You know why you always stare at my ass, don't you? It's the only difference between me and her," she sticks her tongue out, well I guess I imagined her doing so, "mine is better," she stands.

"Vanish, be gone foul wench."

"You're not crazy John, just a jackass," she turns away, I stare at her beaut' of a boot as she takes a few steps towards the door and disappears.

Talking to yourself is always good therapy, especially when you try to see how you look through another person's eyes. Just don't let anyone see. Back to the bedroom, I lay down next to my old friend. She's so beautiful, I begin running my fingers through her hair. She sighs and snorts, her eyelids press tight and her nose twitches. Ooh, she's waking up.

"Hmmmm?"

"Honey?"

"What!" she lunges forward pulling the sheet over her chest. "No! no-no-no-no-no-no, no!" why so many 'no's?

"Rachel, what's wrong?" I rub her back trying to comfort her.

"What do you mean what's wrong? I'm a fucking cheater!" she starts slapping the mattress over and over, "I'm so fucked, that's 'what's wrong' I'm the worst," she covers her eyes, shaking her head.

"Not even in the top million my sweets."

"I betrayed Max," so? "threw away my marriage."

"Did you?" I sit up.

"Yes, no wait no, yes I don't know," see what I mean about persuasion being powerful, simple questions my friend, simple questions... "No, no... you drugged me, rape!"

"What? You bitch. Why the fuck... "

"Shut up, I'm just fucking with you, trying to lighten the mood, ah-ha-ha calm me down, you know," she gets out of bed and starts getting dressed.

What the hell kind of joke is that... well, I guess one I would make, "how can I help? I mean what do I do?"

"Nothing, do nothing for me, forever. This never happened, and I never ran into you," whoa no.

"Hey, hey, I don't want to leave you. Eight years was hell I can't wait another two."

"Two?"

"Until Maxi's cold in the ground," she stares blainkly at me, hides a half smile by shaking her head no.

"You don't get to make jokes like that."

"It ain't a joke if it's accurate. Cuddle time?"

"You're awful," she whips my pants at me.

"No, pretending that you care about some guy because you fucked up his life over a decade ago, that's awful. Stop being a fucking martyr."

"What?" I put my hands on her shoulders, hunch over a little, widening my eyes.

"Grab hold of your fucking life and take responsibility."

"Asshole," she grunts, avoiding eye contact.

"You whore. Don't put your shit on me!" she turns her back to me, my arms drop and she starts walking around my room, getting the remainder of her things, "you're the one who cheated, not only cheated but spent the majority of your day in bed with me. I didn't make you do anything you didn't want to, and sister you wanted to do a whole lot of crazy shit. You want to leave then go, I have shit to do, and I assume you do too. So I suggest you tell him asap, it'll save you some time before you hit that point of unfuckability"

She squints her eyes, puckers her lips and sits on the corner of my bed. She's quiet, and that is the optimum reaction for our current position, it'll allow her to think, look at her you can actually see the gerbil turning the wheel. Self-reflection is key to a happy life, to quote Oscar Wilde 'to love oneself is the beginning of a lifelong romance.' I have to wait this out it can take hours or even days for the reality of the situation sink in.

"Jack," or a couple minutes, "what do we do?" so I have to sit down and comfort her, weird it's actually at my place, but I can't say 'let's talk about this somewhere else,' so I guess we're doing this here and we're holding hands now, what's all this then? Her eyes are open wide, pupils dilated, they look so empty.

"Honey," honey? "I can't tell you what's going to happen, if I can be honest which I'm pretty sure I have been up to this point, an ass albeit but an honest one at that."

"Right," I half expected that to be a whimper or nod not a definite affirmation of understanding, what's your game? Maybe shes just agreeing that I've been an ass.

"All I can say is that I don't know what's over that hill."

"What if I don't tell him?" she looks down at our hands, I think she wants to keep me on the side.

"Then that will be your choice, but it'll eat at you."

"Why?" She sniffles, wipes her eyes and turns her head to give me a mischievous smirk, a smile that looks like she's never been kind before.

"Because you're human: you feel, and have a soul, and a good heart, and you, believe it or not, are a good person, even after all this you're still far better than I," her half grin drops and humanity come to the surface.

"Does it eat at you?"

"Do you really want to know?" she stares deep into my eyes as if looking for something, anything; she shuts her eyes and quickly turns away.

"No."
I pat her hand gently, kiss it, return it to her lap, and wait for her to speak.

"Why would I do something so stupid?"

"Gee thanks," ha-ha I made you giggle. "Good to see you smile," I nudge my knee against hers.

"Thanks," come closer, come closer, kiss me, please God, kiss me… and we have tongue. God damn it. "Are you going to get that?" Damn phone.

"Nah, it's not important," damn it Michelle, you weren't supposed to text until Monday at the earliest.

"Check it."

"No."

She grits her teeth and deepens her voice, "Jack, answer it," she digs her thumbnail into the palm of my hand.

"Ok, ok."

Now to the text: *Hey… I know this is not one of our safe days but meet me somewhere tonight. At midnight, we need to talk*

*Michelle, terrible timing, not today or tonight,*

"So… when?"

"Eh?"

"I can clearly see your text, when will you meet her?"

"Whenever, I'm here for you now."

"Is that a courtesy you extend to every notch on your belt or am I just something special?" she stands up.

"Rachel. Of course you're special."

"Sure."

"I've known you forever; church, school, this isn't just a fling."

"*Yeah…*"

"Rachel…"

"How can I be so sure? How?" how does one say I love you without saying it?

"Look, on the key hook."

"What?"

"By the door, in the living room. Go, go look on the first hook," she walks out of my room, my bedroom door creeks and closes behind her, it stays open just a crack. I close my eyes and listen to her steps, thinking she just might leave. I listen for a jiggle of a doorknob, a clicking of a latch. I listen to nothing. I imagine her out there standing at the door, she strokes the first hook, looks back at the bedroom door that rest lightly on the frame, she grabs it and I hear her walking back.

"Why do you still have this?" her voice is gentle, higher and trembling a little, I don't know if she's holding back tears, laughter, or what. I open my eyes.

It was a gift from her, though I am not the quire boy I once was and I may not know how I currently feel about the almighty, if there is one, I did and have kept faith in one thing. That is my affection for my Rachel Almeida. Easter Sunday the year we entered high school she called me over after mass, we were too old to participate in the egg hunt, but cousins and other little relatives made it an obligation to stay. If the father had a picture into my mind when I was around Rachel he would have had the monsignor on the phone in a heartbeat and I would have been carried off by some special anti-coital sect of the Swiss guards, locked away and have spent the remainder of my days down in the catacombs of the Vatican. I digress. She pulled from her purse an egg painted in four colors: the top was red, the second layer orange, the third purple, and the bottom was black.

"How old are you?" I asked fondling the egg, I remember the bottom feeling chipped and rough.

"It's a gift for you."

"An egg on Easter? Well... far be it from me to disrespect your strange customs. I am honored," I bowed, "thank you my liege."

"Shut up John."

"Let..."

"... me be *frank* the name is yada-yada-yada just open it."

"It's a hardboiled egg."

"Maybe there's something inside it."

"An engagement ring?" I rose on my tiptoes, leaned into her, bumping shoulder to shoulder.

"I'm not the marrying type Jack. After all this time I thought you would have known that by now," I start cracking the egg. At the bottom of the shell, a hole was cut, spackled over then painted black. There was a slit in the whites where something was crammed in.

"I don't think I am either," I say casually while tearing into the meat. It was a small wooden cross coated in crumbs of dry yolk. The majority of the cross is painted black, it has a bat signal carved in the intersection painted yellow.

"Look on the back," she said.
The vertical wood piece was engraved. It read *Sanctum Crucem, Batman* which as any old school Cathy knows means *Holy crucifixion, Batman*. I would obviously cherish this stupid bit of sacrilege for years to come. To this very day, I wear it every Easter. And now I hope Rachel knows my sense of sentimentality when it comes to the subject of her.

"How can you be sure? The truth is you can't. But you can try to trust me or just try to be my friend."

"Yeah," she nods with a few tears and a sniffle.

"If you want me out of your life then I guess I have no choice," I pause, look down then back up with my arms spread out, "I'm gonna have to go on a killing spree or take a senator hostage or something," she laughs, a squeaky outburst forces me to join in.

"Listen Jack..." she began to speak. This conversation goes for another hour resulting in many hugs, several kisses, me getting slapped, the rehashing of our adolescent jokes and this one truism, "I saw you yesterday, I saw you and pulled you over, your blinker wasn't on that long," I knew it! "I just needed to talk to someone. What the fuck? All Max and I talk about is how much I screwed him out of a decent life, he made his own choices. And, my God, just blathering on about the stupidest shit from comedians and shows that were on when I was like two. He hates me a little, I know it."

"No, he doesn't."

"Yes, he does. It's ok. I knew it was a bad idea to say 'hi' the second I tricked the sirens."

"It wasn't bad, I would have done the same thing in your situation."

"Fucked over the person that was there for you, supported you, when you needed them most?" hey, wasn't that me for a while?

"No, to break free from the guilt, how long have you been married a year, year and a half?"

"Three and a half," holy shit.

"I thought you said you ran into him about four years ago?"

"I did."

"Shit you move fast."

"Yeah," she zones out staring at the floor.

"Are you alright? Want water or something?" she sniffles, brushes the tip of her nose with the back of her hand and shakers her head 'no.'

She's quiet for a bit, "you know, sometimes I think I hate him other times I don't and know exactly why I married him but most of the time when I see him, when I see that... that... face, the reasons are just gone," I start rubbing her thigh, I want to tell her 'it's ok' so bad, "I just wish he were dead," wow those are some pretty strong words, I stop rubbing.

"You don't mean that."

"No, but it would make things so much easier, he's the saddest man I know... next to you."

"What?" she wraps her arms around me, driving her head in my shoulder nuzzling, possibly wiping her nose on my shirt.

"I missed you."

"I'll get you home now," you crazy bitch.

"Can't I just stay here? I don't want to see him," no, you'll do me in too you psycho.

"No, you need to see him and talk about this. You said he's forgiving, I'm not saying he'll understand, or he won't be pissed, but at least your conscience will be clear."

She's coated in tears nodding her head; eyes puffy, partially closed, her cheeks red, brow crunched. Is it sick I think she looks really cuddly right now? I help her onto her feet and walk her to the door.

**Friday, 6:55pm, The Deal**

We're in the car. Yes, I'm driving her home. I... am driving her home. At my place she asked for a screwdriver, we walked out to her car. She lifted the hood to get at the battery, popped the bolt off the terminal, threw it in a storm drain and called a friend with a tow truck to bring it home. I called a cab to the impound lot and rescued my baby, she came with, and now I'm out two hundred dollars, that's just great. She hasn't said a word since we left the tow yard, just looking out the window leaning on her arm half on earth, half in hell, pondering the 'numerous' outcomes. It looks like she's on the nineteenth scenario or so, in reality there are only like three if that.
A. She doesn't tell him right away, and it eats away at her until one day he does some insignificant thing that for some reason will annoy the piss out of her. She'll explode in a white rage yelling at him every delightful detail. And it will destroy the geezer, as he sits cowering in fear and rage, feeling humiliated she'll grab her coat and storm out the door.
B. She tells him right away, they fight, she tells him she needs time to think and goes to a relative's place; when she comes back, they'll ignore what happened and slowly drift apart.
C. She tells him and he dies.
 Just playin'. C. He throws her out, and she blames me. I am going to get blamed regardless either for 'pursuing' her, or just the act, such is the fate of the other guy. No matter what I do, no matter how nice I am, I just can't catch a break.

"Jack, I want you to know I don't blame you," why the fuck can't I get a read on you!

"Ok, thank you hun," hun? What's with me and the pet names?

"I'm going to tell him," damn right you will.

"Whatever you think is best."

"I just want one favor?" here we go.

"Yes?"

"We sit and have lunch tomorrow, you still owe me that."

"We're here."

"You can pick the place," she puts her hand on my thigh.

"We are here."

"Do we have a deal?"

"I have your number," I mumble.

"What was that?" she squeezes; digging her fingertips in between the muscles of my inner thigh and pulling up, the pain is excruciating, but I can't show that I'm hurt. I bite my lip, she squeezes harder.

"Ow, ow, fuck," I'm in love.

"Jack I will set him after you right now, so do we have a deal?" I kicked his ass before. I can take him again.

"I got your number."

I left her at the door and drove off. I'm sorry I can't stay to watch the fireworks, but if he sees me he's bound to take her gun and start firing, also I have some things to take care of. First, I have to go to the pub in case Grace shows. I have to leave this one alone. She is pure, she is off limits. Then call the club to see if I still have a job after I apparently went balls to the walls crazy. Last, set up a rendezvous with my lawyer, I need someone to calm my nerves, if he can't meet me then at least a phone call. It's not a lot, but it's crucial that your beloved narrator does not go to the slammer permanently.

**Friday, 7:42pm, Saving Grace**

Why am I doing this? I hate breaking a promise; it's one of my pet peeves. Even if I only half-heartedly agreed to the terms. If I said I will then I must. A man has to have his convictions. To stand for something gives those of us without value in this world something to be proud of. With this said I don't have to be nice to her. I don't have to be in a positive state of mind, or even put in effort to be good company. Hell, I could spit in her eye and call her Fanny and I'd still have kept my word. I merely have to show up roughly around the time I said I'd be there and say 'hi,' if she doesn't show, all the better.

I pull in to a space in front of the F.U.C. hoping she decided not to show and I can get back to what's really important, Rachel I'm sorry I left you alone in the woods to die. I walk inside not looking around, keeping my eyes fixed on the bar, on the same seat from last night. I'm hoping if she's here she won't see me and I can get the bartender to be my witness. I pop my collar and keep my head down slithering towards the bar and take a seat. The tender turns around, good Michael is working again.

"Black Russian?" he asks.

"G&T, London dry, any brand."

"Bad day?" he starts making my drink; a single lime wedge, a single shot of gin from the well, fistful of ice, and tops with tonic.

"You wouldn't believe," I'm invisible to everyone but Michael, "hey, if that old bastard ever shows in here again never let on that you know me, if he asks. Say last night was the first time you ever saw me, you don't know me."

"I don't know you," he slides me my drink.

"Exactly."

"Weirdo," he walks way.

If she does see me, I'll be on my way. I'll tell her something came up and I have to go, I know she would be better off if I leave now and never come back. I'm just a stranger. Just someone passing through. If she wants to have a drink too bad, I'm driving, one is enough for me. Please, please don't show. I sip on my glass. The clock above my head slows every time I bring the glass to my lips, have I even put the drink on the counter? Move faster, I can't be here forever. I'm half way down the skin of the lime; it's been about three minutes, that's long enough to claim attendance. At the bottom of this cup holds my peace, my freedom, the tart citrus taste calms me down, and the bitterness of the tonics wakes me up. I put the cool glass on my forehead as I reach for my wallet. The ice and sweat of the glass is the only thing that can settle this headache, why am I so nervous? I put down a ten, stand and ready to leave when I feel a gentle pinch on the back of my neck, I have been discovered.

"My hero," God damn it Grace. Why couldn't her guy just have shown up? She's all gussied up, I hope she didn't do that for me.
I glare at her and say nothing, she leans into the stool next to me and starts swiveling.

"So how goes it?" I clear my throat and fix my jacket.

"I'm sorry, but I have to go," my rasp breaks with a squeak or two, taking away the air of seriousness I was trying to convey.

"Mark... you just got here, you promised me," Mark? Oh yeah.

"I promised I'd be here and I kept it," give her a smile, gently brush her cheek, talk slow, show her who you are, "I never said anything about staying," a complete asshole.

"That's not fair," she pouts her lip, don't play these cutesy guilt games. You're an adult, act like it.

"Life's not fair. Look I'm going to be straight with you, I don't know what you saw in me last night but that was a lapse in character, heat of the moment shit, ya'know. I am the architypal bastard and this," I bat my finger back and forth between us, "what I'm doing now, pushing you away. Trust me, this is the nicest thing I can possibly do for you."

"Then why did you come?"

"Cus' I promised you. I may be a dick, but I'm an honest one."

"Good, I like honesty," God did I come off this needy?

"No. Just no, I'm a bad guy," she laughs.

"Come on Mark," she touches my shoulder.

"Don't touch me. Listen, I was only interested in you last night because you sat alone, I thought you'd be easy. When you rejected me you instantly stopped being worth my time."

"Then why did you want to see me again."

"I didn't, that's my point. I struck a deal so you'd let me go. Think a trapped coyote chewing its paw off. I only came to fulfill my obligation, so consider yourself fulfilled. I mean what the hell happened to your guy? He wasn't nice enough? Too ugly? What?"

"I don't know what you're talking about, I was alone all night. 'My guy' didn't even show, well he doesn't sound too good to me," she nervously laughs, who was that guy staring at us?

"Don't lie, I saw him right before those assholes went all guns a-blazin'. I saw him standing in the doorway looking us over last night, he was staring right at you."

"What guy?" I start looking around behind her.

"That guy," I point to an empty table, she turns around, and I sneak away.

"You're an asshole!" not the first person to call me that today.

"I warned you," she follows me to my car.

"Why then, just why?"

"Why what?"

"You saved me?"

"How shitty are the people you know? How is me moving you away from gun fire akin to flirting? I don't have to be in love with you to not want you dead. And they weren't even shooting at us, you know that, right? They were just some jag offs who finally found out how to twiddle their dicks. I freaked out and ran. I'm sorry if you got the wrong idea of me."

"What happened?"

"I just fucking explained it, listen."

"No, to you?" she brushes my cheek. "You were nice and charming last night, why then and not now?" I grab her hand, pull it off my face and drop it.

"What do you want me to say? Oh lord-e-lord I have seen the error of my ways, and now I've come to repent. No, I just wanted to fuck you! Ok, I didn't want to say it, I was trying to be nice," I open my door, she pushes it closed. Don't touch my shit.

"You could have, you still can. What changed?" the chips in the paint are showing. She reeks of desperation.

"Stuff happens and... I can't. Lets' leave it at that."

"What stuff? You married?"

"Nope, don't even have a gal pal. Good bye," she leans her back against my door so I can't get in.

"Then what? I mean is there something wrong with me?" she spreads her arms and looks down at herself.

"You want to know?"

"Yeah, I feel I deserve to know."

"Deserve, that's a pretty strong opinion," I grab her by the arm and show her our reflection in my window.

"Let go."

"Look here. Now, other than my crappy car what do you see?"

"Us..." she brushes my hand off her bicep, looks at me with her mouth partially open, and looks back at our reflection, "where are you going with this?"

"Nowhere you want, just...just look at you. You're a good girl. You're pretty, you read, you think. I mean look at what you're wearing; a white cardigan, blue dress. Last night you were all dressed up for some guy you wanted to meet, you hoped to meet. And again with me, some random jag off, you've dressed to impress. You're a doll. Now look at me and what do you see?" she looks long and hard at my reflection.

"It's not a trick question; my clothes, my face, I look like a mess. I'm greasy, unshaven, eyes half bloodshot, ratty broken nails stained black with mud and blood. I look like I crawled out of a shallow grave. How can you want this?"

"Mark..." she touches my shoulder and I explode.

"Right there, right fucking there! I already lied to you," I show her my license, "now you see!" I point at myself, "I'm an asshole, that's who I am."

"Why would you lie about your name?" it doesn't even faze her.

"Because I wanted to get away from you as fast as I could, the less you know about me the better."

"Why?" she yells, starts getting in my face too, "huh? What's so God damn bad about you?" she pokes me in the chest, from my sternum a blunt pain begins to radiate around her finger.

"I will fuck you up," I grab her finger and toss her hand, "that's why, because I will hurt you," I say more forcefully feeling the peircing talons of something uncontrolable, undescribable, clawing its way up from inside me.

"How?" her voice gets quiet, monotone.

"If I had an extra hour last night, oh lass, an extra hour and I could have done so much," I pause panting from frustration, "I'd have gone with you. Rip your clothes off with my teeth. I would've turned you in and ate you out, I'd 'ave fucked you six ways to Sunday. Kink, crushed, bound, bitten; I'd give you it all. Then as you rested in your post coital-coma, poof," I poke her on the forehead, "I'd disappear. Gone to work or my place or something then screw the next needy bitch I came across, I just don't care anymore."

"Oh, really?" her arms cross and she tilts her head, from prep to punk in less than five seconds.

"Yes, and maybe I keep in contact. Keep you on a string, to play with for a month or two. Tell you I love you, hold you tight. Make you really believe it, believe me, trust me. But the second I get bored I'm gonzo. I'm not a hundred percent on how things would play out; a fight, a scene, a pic with someone else, I don't know but I'm sure you'd hate yourself after, and I'll laugh and laugh and laugh," I can see horror slowly take over her composure, "you drive me fucking crazy! And I just met you. If we screwed, I'd have to fight off the urge to strangle you in your sleep just so I wouldn't have to put up with that needy whine in the morning. You are so God damn pathetic it makes me want to pour acid in your eyes, cut out your tongue and run you over!" she's frozen, sick, pale, looking weak and holding her gut but her eyes are still full of rage. She's trying to stand her ground, "I wanted to do one good thing in my life, one fucking thing!" I'm yelling in her face, she's backing away from me slowly, "I wanted to leave one dumb cunt alone. The only reason I came here was to say you're better off forgetting me. Now you've gone and fucked that up. Thanks a lot," I push her shoulder, she falls on her ass and bursts into tears, "God damn it! What!" I wish they shot her.

"What do you mean 'what'?" she screeches, "you're being awful!" am I?

"Yeah? Good, learn. People are shit, and no one is going to tell you that straight. Hate me, despise me but never say I didn't warn you of what's out there," warn you of things like me.

"Why are you being so mean?" she lays down on the sidewalk blubbering, her stockings are tearing on her right thigh, she's kicking her legs scratching the points of her red pumps. "I just wanted a drink," I think I may have actually broken her.

"Was that really necessary?" a woman's voice asks. It's not hers', I look around, and I don't see any one. My adrenaline drops and a cold sweat comes up, my stomach turns. I crouch and try to assist the slimy child up when she lunges at me violently.

"No! No! You don't get to touch me."

"Fine," I stand to leave.

"No!" rolling onto her stomach she grabs hold of my leg tightly with both arms. The wind blows up her dress exposing her white granny-panties spotted with little cartoon cat heads. Comedy is tragedy times time and in this case two seconds is long enough. I cover my mouth trying to hold back my laughter, then shake off her grip and get in my car. This is me being kind. I looked at her lying on the sidewalk, she rolled on to her back again hiding her shame, holding her stomach with one hand and with the other wiping away tears and snot from her face. She stood as soon as I tricked the ignition. I drive off and through my side mirror I see her run back into the bar hunched over, her arms well below her hips, hands pressing her skirt to her legs. She's walking to the wolves, I hope this time wiser than before. This is me being kind.

### Friday, 8:25pm, Guilt

The most natural response to pain is avoidance; the zebra flees from the lion, the addict grasps at their closest fix. Numbing yourself is the best form of protection when the shit hits the fan. I have no want to feel, but when confronted with situations such as these it's hard not to feel at least a little guilty. I'm sitting in my car; my head pressed on the steering wheel, it has been for a while. My legs are beginning to fall asleep. I have to go in. I have to, if not for my sanity then at least for my legs. I bang my head on the wheel and punch the dash. "Mother Fuckers!" I yell, I shut off the engine and unbuckle, it's time. The door opens. The ice cold air hits and chills the tears in my eyes. I'm scared shitless at what could happen.

"Hello," she said not making eye contact.

"Hi, Johnathan Klaus here to see a Fredrich of the same surname. He was brought in sometime last night. Something about a bar brawl?"

I can be deceptive if need be. I just don't get any thrill out of lying, it takes away from the game, but you do what you have to I suppose. I convinced her I was Freddie's brother. He left the ICU six hours ago and was moved to room 322. Fredrich is out cold; his face torn to shit, his head wrapped in bandages, left eye is covered, possibly gone, right forearm in a cast. His left cheek: the little skin that is exposed has a huge purple splotch with a yellow center scabbing over. His mouth is all messed up: he's missing some teeth, the rest are shattered, his bottom lip is stitched on, and his top one is cut down the middle partially separating his philtrum. I took the chair next to his bed. My God, what have I done?

"You know I'm sorry about this, I… I don't know what to say. Fred, can I call you Fred?" he's out, "I'll call you Fred. Usually when I fuck a person over they don't know it or if they do it's on a much smaller scale, emotional you know. Can you hear me? Hello. I uh… I hope you can. I don't remember what happened, you probably don't either. Ahhh I'm an ass. I guess it doesn't matter if I remember, it's still my fault. Look man I'm incredibly sorry. I wouldn't wish this on my worst enemy. You have to believe this wasn't me. Not that it wasn't me, I mean I'm not like that. Wake up! Say something, please anything. Spit in my eye, call the cops. Please let me know there's something in there," when all else fails there are no atheists in hell. "Omnipotent and eternal God, the everlasting salvation of those who believe, hear us on behalf of Thy sick servant, Fredrich Klaus, for whom we beg the aid of Thy pitying mercy, that, with his bodily health restored, he may give thanks to Thee… Omnipotent and eternal God, the everlasting salvation…"

"Fuck you," well he's alive. That's something.

"Hello?"

"Who the fuck are you?"

"I'm…"

"Where am I?"

"The hosp…"

"And why the hell are you here?"

"You're ill, I thought…"

"You thought wrong boy, I ain't sick. I'm hurt and that doesn't give you the right to fucking walk in and start with that voodoo shit," can I get a word in?

"It was a psalm," I'm speaking quietly so not to aggravate him anymore.

"Whatever," ok then, now it's time for me to leave. I stand. "No, I'm sorry man sit. My mouth always pisses people off. I ain't got a filter," no kiddin'.

"I'm sorry."

"Don't be it's my fault, probably why I'm in here."

"You don't remember what happened to you? How can you be so sure it's your fault?"

"Nah, I probably ticked off some short fuse, it wouldn't be the first time. So who are you?"

"Does it matter? I saw a person in need."

"What are you like a saint or something?" he chuckles, a little blood sprays from a popped stitch in the corner of his mouth.

"Way off. I have enough stories of debauchery and perversion to turn your stomach."

"An example?"

"Oh lord-e-lord what do you want? Funny? Crazy? Scary? I could give you an alphabetized list."

He looked down and thought for a while.

"What's the strangest story you got? Let's start there," he turns his head to look at me. His eye swollen, the thin slit only shows pupil. I smile, I feel nauseous but still I smile. I rub my hands together as they float between my thighs and nod trying to hold back the shivers and a look of fear and revoltion.

"I have a lot of 'em, give me a letter."

"C."

"Well then, C... C... Oh! That would be the curious case of the cock killing crapper."

"What?" he looks disgusted, or maybe that's just the only face he can make.

"A little alliteration: catchy right? Sounds like a Sherlock Holmes story, at least I think so."

"No, God no, the hells wrong with you?"

"No, it's not as gross as it sounds. Long story short I was about to cum when she yelled 'I gotta shit' and I stopped. My first thought, for some reason, was that she wanted to do a Boston steamroller on me. I don't know why it was, it's not my thing, she's never done that to me before. So I stopped and stared at her for a minute thinking to myself '*do you want me to lay down?*' I don't know. My face must have tipped her off or something, she knew I was close; she just didn't want me to blow my load early. Her thought: wrecked the mood then switched position and continue."

"Changed position before or after?"

"Before or after what?"

"She shit."

"Dude pay attention, she didn't really have to shit. She just wanted to slow me down."

"Ah, it's still messed up."

"There's more to the story; a vibrating egg rammed up her ass and some piss play," his head jolts back, "I just gave you the short and currlies. Hey, don't blame me, you wanted to know."

"Yeah... yeah I did," he got quiet, looking down. Silence, times passing and he won't look at me. I'm staring at the small stream of blood coming from his mouth forming a droplet on his chin, now I'm starting to get worried that he's remembering what happened. He wipes his chin and takes a deep breath in, "do you believe in God?"

"I was just reciting a blessing, a psalm, what do you mean do I believe in God?"

"Do you believe in God?"

"I like to think I do."

"Thinking ain't the same as actually having faith," he takes off his blanket, his legs are cut up and bruised, he has a welt on his left shin about the size of a clementine.

"Do you?"

"Of course I do, I wouldn't be alive if I didn't," he pulls out his morphine drip, the tearing and visceral slap sound of the tape and needle coming off his arm echoes in my head.

"What are you doing?" he sits up. I'm freaking out a little, readjusting myself in my seat.

"What does it look like?" he moves his legs to the edge of the bed.

"A lot of bad ideas," he drops his feet to the ground, "you're really going to hurt yourself."

"Stand kid, stand," I do, and he starts using me for ballast, he dips first then straightens out.

"What's happening?"

"Can't you see?" he takes a few steps away.

"No."

"I'm alive," he turns off the tv and walks back to me.

"Yes, I can see that."

"And I forgive you," he holds on to me by my arms.

"What?"

"Don't act stupid. You know I'm just saying what you want to hear."

"What?" silence: no beeping monitors or flat lines, nobody walking in the hall. All that exists at this moment is the slow thumping of my heart, with each beat I am thrown back as if someone were to punch me in the stomach over and over again, in the same spot, in that un-halting rhythm.

"I'm brain damaged man, dead head. I'm out, and I'll most likely always be. I'd be lucky enough to sound like a retarded six-year-old having a spaz attack let alone stand and walk with ease."

"This is real, don't fuck with me. This is real," I back a way a little, a few tears cloud my vision and my foot hits the leg of the chair, I look down then look back up at him slowly approaching me. His arm extended, reaching out to my shoulder.

"No John."

"This isn't funny. Jack, my name is Jack, I'm Jack!"

"Recap, what were you doing before I woke up?"

"Pray…"

"Praying? How many times?" his voice changed, its identical to mine.

"Two, three."

"Your head bowed, you can't remember. John, you passed out in the chair next to me around the sixteenth recital. And when you wake up you're going to cry and you're going to wish that you were dead but you shouldn't. Never wish that."

"Why?"

"Well, it'll kill me too for one."

"That's a bit selfish."

"Exactly," he said with a finger point and a wink (or blink I can't tell with only one eye showing).

He fades away, the room started to shake, and I'm thrown into the chair behind me. A nurse with her head down comes in and walks up to me, she removes her nursing cap and lets her long red locks drop to her shoulders. It is imaginary Jamie. She sits in my lap, her legs crossed hanging over the armrest, and she brushes her pointer finger down from my brow to the tip of my nose.

"We meet again, Jacky boy. You might have finally gotten what you wanted."

"No, I just want to wake up."

"Your wish is my command, love," she kisses me softly, her hand cradling my face, her finger pressing into my temple.

I woke in the chair a little before eleven, still feeling the warmth of Jamie's hand on my face and the pain of her finger fiddling with my brain. Fredrich is still out. I sat up leaning over the bed, covered my mouth and let out a muddled bellow then began to cry, he is my brother now. Using my tears, I decided to make the cross on his bandaged forehead.

*"In nomine Patris et Filii et Spiritus Sancti. Fratris meus es,"* I stand to go take a piss in his bathroom. I readjust myself, and as I leave, I take one last look back at Freddie. Jamie has taken my seat at his side.

"You'll look after him?"

"Always."

**Friday, 11:07pm, Confession**

I close the door and start walking. I can hear the steps of a young woman down the hall past the corner, by the partially muddled sound I'd say she's hugging the wall and walking a little too quickly. By the sound I can deduce she's about five-five, five-six. She's moving faster as she gets closer to the corner and on the turn she's going to run into me. Prepare for impact in T-minus five, four, three, two, oh. She drops a folder and quickly bends down to pick it up. She's a nurse and fairly pretty, her hair is a dark brown pinned up under the cap, but from what little that does show it's very curly, her white uniform hugs her body tightly. She's left handed, her name tag is on her right breast. Her skin is a light brown-bronze and smooth, her nose is small and thin as are her lips, and she has relatively high cheekbones. Her eyes are a mix between brown and hazel, and she wears no makeup, not that she needs any, she just looks the type to wear at least a little blush or eyeliner everywhere she goes.

"I'm sorry," she has a hint of an accent; she gives me a smile, "family?" I'm melting over the dimples in her cheeks.

"Uhhh... What?"

"Of a patient, are you family?"

"Oh, yes Freddie. I'm the brother," I shake her hand, "how will he be?" Her smile drops.

"Freddie...Klaus?"

"That is he, yes," she stops making eye contact and shakes her head. I'm scared.

"I'm so sorry," she comes in for a hug, a bit too close but why not, "I don't know what to tell you."

"Just tell me he'll be alright," wrapped in my arms and hanging off my neck she looks deep into my eyes, she shakes her head again, "will he live?"

"Honey, that would be the worst thing for him. No one should have to live like that, I hope they hang the bastard who did this to him," now this is getting awkward. She stops hugging

"I wouldn't blame him, I blame the situation."

"What do you mean?"

"Freddie has always been a little short tempered add drinks and a fight is inevitable."

"Didn't you see him, that wasn't a fight it was a **Blud-Ge-O-Ning**," she fummbles a little on the pronunciation, over emphasizing every paired letter.

"My brother loves to fight, God when we were kids we got into scrapes all the time," she nods her head making some 'uh-huh' hums, "once we fought about who was king of the mountain, we were in our treehouse, and I was close to the window. He punched me in the gut, I kick him in the crotch then he pushed me, and I stumbled and fell out. I fractured my ulna in three places that day," raising my arm rotating it. Laughing.

"Oh my goodness," I chuckled at her reaction.

"Yeah, I blame the booze, I blame the city, but I don't blame him or the other guy."

She and I talked for a little while; I told her some stories of my faux childhood. She laughed at all of them and comforted me with every sigh I made. I felt my life getting longer with each exhale. Every time I opened my mouth I grew a year older, every lie I told she felt closer to me. I was the distraught brother, hopeless, burying myself in memories. We sat on the floor down the hall of my brothers' room, I shed a few tears, and I could see she felt my pain.

"Do you want to stay the night?"

"I can't, it's breaking my heart seeing him now. I don't think I can wake up to that little ball of crazy bound and bandage."

"I understand," she kisses my cheek, "I'm sorry, you're probably going through a lot right now."

"I don't even know you name."

"Can't you read?" pointing at her badge, I can read it. I just can't pronounce it.

"I want you to tell me your name," she giggles.

"It's Nereida."

"Nereida" I repeat, "that's pretty."

"What's yours?"

"John, but everybody knows me as Jack."

"Jack. Thank you."

"Nereida."

"I wish there was more I could do."

134

"It's alright. I'm not much of a brother, I got used to being alone. Now I finally am."

"Jack."

"Yes."

"I've been off work for the past twenty minutes."

"Oh, I'm sorry. I'll let you go, thank you for sitting with me," I attempt to stand, she holds me down.

"Don't apologize," she grabs my hand, "follow me," she stands and begins walking.

Nereida took me into the elevator and hit the ground floor, as we dropped she removed her cap and crocs. Letting down her curly hair and wiggling her toes in freedom. The bell sounds for floor two. She tilts her head releasing the stress in her neck and shoulders, if I was feeling well I would try to kiss her beautiful neck. I have never liked elevators, they tend to disrupt my stomach; I don't get motion sickness in cars, plains, trains or boats but in an elevator my mind's a mile long and my stomach is a pound heavier. I force myself into a corner and grip the rails. She looks at me.

"Are you alright?"

"I tend to use the stairs."

"Aw, honey you should have told me."

"It's fine. We're almost there," we hit the ground and the door opens, she exits, but I stay behind.

"Come on," she motions, again I follow.

"So where are we going?"

"Nowhere special, just come."

She brings me into the breakroom. It's small; the walls are white with a thick blue line running horizontally in the middle, there's a square wooden table's in the center with a plastic cup half full of water on the furthest most corner. The counter running from the door to the fridge holds a microwave, coffee maker, and both sugar and cream caddies. There are two doors in the back of the room just past the fridge, one with the male symbol the other directly across with the female, she walks me into the ladies room.

In the locker room, I, unsure what to do, stand in the doorway as she tricks the lights, there are only a few rows. The actual lockers are all blue, the benches in each row set I assume

at one point were painted blue as well, the wood has obviously
been worn and sanded but the ends are still colored. The shower
station is in the front right next to the bathroom, and in the back,
there's a fire exit. We're alone. She brings me to her locker,
takes out a key from her pocket, it's on one of those pink coil
chains. She opens the lock, pops the door and begins undressing.
I turn away for modesties sake.

"Are you alright?"

"I'm fine, I mean, I don't think the shock has hit me
quite yet," she's standing in her bra and panties pulling out her
street clothes.

"I'm so sorry, please look at me," she has a decent body,
very gentle features, I would love to brush my lips over her hip
bone, still I find all this strange. "I just want you to feel
comforted," she puts her pants on, "I mean you just pretty much
lost your brother, and you probably don't think I understand,"
she approaches me.

"I try not to assume, it leads to too many assumptions."

"Clever, I like that. I do know what you're going
through, I lost my sister a while back. I know what it's like to
suddenly be your parents' favorite," I'm trying so hard to not to
look at her tits.

"I'm sorry, what happened?"

"It was years ago."

"I'm sure you still remember, it's alright if you don't
want to tell me."

"No, it's fine. I don't really know what happened. I
know she killed herself, but it was back home, so the details
were muddled when they got to me".

"I'm sorry, where's home?"

"The Cape"

"Cod?"

"No, Verde," that explains the accent.

"How long you've been here?"

"Since I was eleven," she comes closer and hugs me,
resting her face on my chest.

"Do you miss your sister?" through my shirt, I can feel a
tear sliding down her cheek

"Mhm…"

"This is a bit weird," she sniffles and looks up at me.

"I know, but I'm trying to help," she ties her hair in a ponytail then puts on deodorant.

"Are we going somewhere?"

"If you want, I don't think you should be alone right now," she puts her shirt on.

"I'm fine, you can stop worrying," she grabs my hand gently and nuzzles it.

"Come with me."

She pulls me into the bathroom, we go into the last stall, and she locks it. She asks me to unzip my fly, I do. She asks if she's beautiful, she is. She kisses me tenderly, I am reminded of the passion I feel whenever I kiss Siobhan and how this is almost the antithesis. Her kiss is soft, passive, my heart is steady. I am at complete ease. She slides her hand down my pants and grabs hold of me, she exposes my dick and nudges me to sit, I sit. She drops to her knees, pulls my pants around my ankles and begins sucking and tugging. She has a light touch and a fluttering tongue. I focus on her head moving up and down, her eyes are closed. Her other hand is cradling my thigh gently. I'm trying not to enjoy this as much as I am but that playful tongue is really making that difficult. She takes her hand off my thigh, and I hear an unzipping sound, then she stops. Nereida pulls from her purse a condom. I roll it on, she removes her pants and takes a seat. I miss the target, we laugh.

"Can you uh… stabilize it?"

"Yeah sure," I hold it straight and slide in. She begins some Kegel-like flexing. I can feel the mouth of her vag squeezing and relaxing, it's an interesting sensation not great but something new. She starts thrusting her hips, slowly at first, kissing my forehead. She leans forward and, putting her hands on the wall, looks down at me and smiles.

"How are you feeling?"

"Good."

"Good?" she starts thrusting harder, "look at me," I see pity in her eyes, "I want you to cum, please cum for me," the sensation is dull. This is too weird.

"I'm trying."

"Don't try, just enjoy," she closes her eyes and continues.

I start looking around the stall. Girls are far less expressive in lavatory banter than men, this great big beige canvas and nothing. In any men's room stall there's always some chicks number, or somebody writing their name and someone else writing next to it *is a faggot*, I miss the classic poem *here I sit broken hearted came to shit but only farted* which is always strategically placed in the third stall if I'm remembering my collegial experience properly. That disgusting creativity is one of the few things I love about my people, it is the truest form of American literature.

I close my eyes, and the clanking of the porcelain fades away. I imagine being in bed with my Joani, the pain behind her eyes that melts away when I show up poolside. That smile she has when she first sees me in front of her, I'm drifting to that place where I feel good for bringing joy to someone just by existing. This is pleasure, Nereida is grunting and groaning on top of me and as beautiful as she is I feel nothing, I'm just about there with Siobhan lying in bed, nuzzling noses, looking deeply into her eyes. Here is where bliss comes, here is where I climax. The balloon tip fills with a quick burst of spunk and Nereida collapses on top of me panting, my face buried in her tits. The warmth of her cotton shirt and steaming sweat feel like they're burning my face, I can hear her heart beat through the padding of her bra and shirt, and for her I don't feel anything.

"Feel better?"

"Much," I say muffled by her clothed breast, she starts to laughs.

"Good, good."

This is where I leave Nereida, or better yet she disassociates herself with me. She gets quiet the second her pants are on and doesn't acknowledge me. She's silent, without emotion. Did she just try to fuck my pain away? Was there something that I did wrong? I feel embarrassed as she gathers her things. I think of my first time as I watching her leave, her not looking back. I didn't feel any bond with her during but now that she's gone I miss her. I feel a little heartbroken over the strangest stranger I've ever met. I rest for a sec and lick my wounds before I get up; I appreciate the bruises on my thigh left by Rachel, put my dick away and leave. I have to hand it to her, I do feel better.

## Friday-Saturday, 1:03am, Shawn to the Rescue

The road between days has become a relaxing place for me. Under the pale maroon sky, I am at complete ease. There's enough traffic on the road to keep me awake, but empty enough for me to have a little fun. A challenger approaches the king, I rev my engine and blow past him. My car may look like a bucket of puke on a hot summer day but it runs better than most. This time, for me at least, seems like a time of great change, not just change from one day to the next, there's something inexplicably new in the air, and I like it.

Once home I suddenly realize it's been a while since I checked my phone. I never go more than twenty minutes without looking at my messages, I open it to see a plethora of 'em. (I always liked that word 'Plethora,' be it the sound or the memory of one of my favorite comedies I try to slip it in whenever I can). Some from the girls I neglected today saying 'How dare you?' or some iteration of that. At least I'm missed by someone. Melony left numerous messages crying that I abandoned her, I listened to one particular voice mail from Mel several times, it was just her yelling at the top of her lungs saying 'exactly like my boyfriend', listing off all my flaws, eventually it just became an unintelligible high-pitched blubber. I got one text from Jamie saying *call me please*, several texts from Shawn asking if I needed his help to call or text before 10 if I want to talk. I found these texts to be calming. Shawn has this amazing ability to make anyone feel comforted no matter how screwed they may be. I sent a text to both Jamie and Shawn: *Could you talk to Joao? I need to keep this job.*

Shawn replied quickly: *Np. I go right now,* but Jamie took a while to get back: *I could, but don't know what he'll do, he's pretty pissed.* I text Jamie: *forget it <3,* I wouldn't want her to deal with that animal any more than need be, and there's always the chance that he'll try something, and then I'll have to kill him. She responded immediately with: *<3<3 Movie sun? maybe dinner?* I agreed. Shawn texted me half an hour later and told me to call João in the morning. *Thanks, can always count on you.* And as one of the craziest days of my life draws to a close I decide to go to sleep before anything else comes up to bite me in the ass. I went to bed with at least a little hope that my life isn't over and as I lay in my bed wrapped in sheets, cuddling a pillow, my phone goes off, I decline. It rings again, so I mute and throw it in the chair near my bed. I need my beauty sleep.

**Saturday, noon, Good Signs**

"I don't want to walk around with a smile a mile long like an idiot just to be blindsided. Look into everything, please… thank you."

I called my old He-bro James Roth esq. from Dartmouth who grew into an extremely vicious lawyer. I asked him to make sure that the case was actually thrown out, he owes me a favor or two, and using his connections he found out there's no record of my time in the pit or of my arraignment and said 'even if I could find your file when a case is thrown out, so long as you don't do anything else stupid, you should be good'. I don't consider the hospital visit stupid. Whooo, I finally feel like things are going my way. I got my lawyer making sure I'm good, I called the Grease-ball, yes I still have a job, Jamie is still down to hang out, I finally nailed Rachel and it's almost time to pay a visit to my lovely Vanessa. I'm on cloud nine. My phone goes off, its Siobhan calling me again. This is like the sixth time today.

"Ciao bella," I say as playfully as possible trying to give a hint of (a tinge of) arrogance to voice my frustration .

"What? Are you alright?" she sound concerned, good.

"Yeah, are you?"

"I've called a few times today, you haven't been answering."

"I know."

"I got worried, I haven't heard from you."

"So? You left me in the tank, what the hell do you care?"

"I know, I fucked up. I called the station yesterday morning, they said you were out."

"Ah, you were worried about little ol' me? Afraid someone else picked my patch?"

"You've been ignoring my calls."

"I think I have the right, I'm still pretty pissed."

"I know, I know and you have every right to be. I just called to make sure you're alright?"

"I am."

"And like I said I just wanted to make sure," she's panicking quietly, he's in the house.

"What did you think happened?"

142

"With you? Anything," I can hear her moving. She's in her room sitting on her bed, she just laid down. I can hear her hair rubbing against the pillows and the receiver, "I'm just glad to hear you're ok," circular conversation, boring.

"Bye."

"Wait, wait. Do you want to come over?" I imagine her sitting up rapidly, readjusting her posture leaning forward and crossing her legs just hoping that I forgive her.

"I can't now," and I can hear air escaping.

"Have a date?" she's partially biting her tongue.

"Good bye Siobhan."

"Joani!"

I stay silent.

"Are we alright? Jack?"

"Time and silence, love, the cure for all ailments."

"What... if... you don't know.... if you went deaf?" she sounds elated; her response is quick, energetic and choppy.

"Clever, see you later Joan."

"Thank you," she has settled down.

I hung up. I find it hard to stay mad at her, no matter what she has or hasn't done. Maybe it's our history, maybe she's the only person I know who's just as lonely as I am. In the end it really doesn't matter, whatever keeps me going back for more she, on some level, is aware of it and knows a phone call alone will solve the problem. I better cheer up before V gets here.

Now Vanessa is kinda different than the rest, not to say they're all the same but they're primarily in similar boats. For instance, she usually comes here for our romps, and her situation is well... she hasn't always been taken per se. Since I first started with her, she has had five failed relationships and for the past two months been engaged. I've been her lover for the better part of three years and apparently her only constant, the key to our success you ask? She knows more about theoretical physics than she does me. I am an enigma, now doesn't that just sound sexy. I'm never jealous when she's gotten herself into something, and she's willing to end a relationship if she feels they lost trust, or are just suspicious of her. As they should be, I mean she's faithless before the first kiss. The doorbell sounds and I stupidly open it without looking through the peephole, no it's not Vanessa. So you have returned to strike me down, beware I will not be taken so easily.

**Saturday, 12:30, Surprise**

To my chagrin, the beautiful vixen who calls upon my door is not the lovely Vanessa but the recently weeping Rachel. My pocket buzzes, that I know in my heart is Vanessa saying something like *can you come here?* Or *my fiancé has questioned me, I can't leave yet* ☺. But yes my true and trusted friend this is Rachel at my door covered in new tears, her makeup running down her cheeks, she's dressed in black jeans, black tank top and a thin charcoal coat carrying a well-packed suitcase. I'm guessing she packed last night and hid it in the closet under some clothes, knowing her ass would be tossed out on the streets as soon as she opened her mouth. So she didn't tell him immediately, she had to be in the mindset. She had to wait for the right time. Imagine the hell she went through lying in bed next to that decrepit body knowing how much pain she'll cause him in a few hours. With each passing minute the guilt had to have been building, driving her crazy, she looks like she hasn't slept a wink, just staring at the clock or at her phone all night long.

With all this said and my sympathy exhausted I must question her reasoning for waiting until the morning, and exactly how she explained her absence yesterday. I'm sorry love I dropped you off to fix this not me, I like the way I'm broken but thanks for your concern. Take care… slam the door. Slam the door. Please God, give me the strength to shut the door in the face of this forsaken woman. Damn it, why the fuck am I doing this?

"What happened?" I lean on the door, not from concern. I'm weak from every fiber of my being fighting against each other as I tried to close that damn door.

"It's over," her face cringes and crinkles, her eyes close, she shakes her head and starts crying. "He said 'that's it', he's had it and just…just kicked me out," a normal reaction I would say. Side note these are the moments you wish people still carried around handkerchiefs, it would be so much more dramatic if she punctuated that pause with a hanky to the mouth or better yet a patting of the eye.

"You're here?" just looking at my phone no big deal: *Can't make it now, come here around 6 ;) I have something to tell you*

"What are you doing?"

"My phone, I wanted to make sure it wasn't important."

"People don't text emergencies," she grabs my phone and throws it onto my loveseat.

"Obviously you've never seen a vegan celeb eating a BLT, what's with the case?"

"He just needs time to think, there's no way he'll just end it. Right?" so you come to the guy you just cheated on him with to give yourself some assurance that your marriage isn't dead, eh? A bit counterintuitive.

"So you barge in and assume that I'll give you asylum," it's a mad house, a mad house!

"I don't assume, I know."

"How?" I am so not sleeping on the loveseat. God damn it, I am not leaving my bed.

"Because you're you," and I'm such a nice guy, right? "And you'll let me stay," she pokes the Bat cross on my neck, I don't even remember putting it on this morning.

"Ok, you may stay for a day or two," she walks in.

"Or three," she mutters under her breath.

"What was that?" I know what you said. Have you the gall to repeat it?

"I said as long as I need," what? "Would be polite to say to your guest."

"You must have other friends, family. I have to know, why here and who's sleeping where?"

"Because you are partially responsible," partially! Ok you got me there, but do I owe you this? I drove you home what more do you want? "And as long as we don't do anything," do you mean bump ugly's? "We may share the bed, but so help me if you try anything you will be on the couch."

"Loveseat."

"Whatever."

"Well, that should be easy."

"What's easy?"

"I'm leaving after five, coming back to ready for work and by the time I get off you'll be sleeping."

She acknowledges that I have a routine, 'same old same old' she spouts, I must have been a real anal prick as a kid. She keeps reminiscing on our childhood; I don't know how she can remember all this shit. I made her lunch out of boredom, nothing special just some chicken soup and a turkey sandwich, she ate it. She said nothing so I can't say if she liked it or not. When she wasn't talking about the good ol'days she was just blankly staring at everything in my place. I don't know what to do about her. She's the saddest person I've ever met. Rachel's only been here for a few hours, but I can't stand her looking at me like I'm a leper. Every time I look over from writing in my diary she's staring at me. She's doing so now, just thinking of how big of a mistake meeting me has been. I don't want to be remembered like this. It's currently three thirty, I have an hour and a half before I gotta leave but I don't know what to do about her when I leave. I tried turning on the tv and acting like we're buddies again, trying to find a movie but what can I put on? Drama? Enough of that. Comedy? Different tastes I like Abbot and Costello and she likes Laurel and Hardy. History? Boring. Tick tock tick tock, Help me?

"So what are you thinking about?" when all else fails, try to listen.

"I don't know, stuff," she mumbles.

"Real descriptive. Come on, you're moping we gotta cheer you up?" I put my arm around her shoulder and pull her in close.

"I guess I'm thinking about…" I have to save you from this. In short, she's thinking about how she screwed up her marriage, her mixed feelings, how sweet I am for opening my doors and that she doesn't know what to do. About what I asked, she doesn't know what to do about anything.

"I'm sorry," I give her a kiss on the cheek, and we hug.

"It's ok," I see the clock on my oven, 5:23. I sit up, stretch, pat her thigh a couple times and rest my hand on her knee.

"Well darling it's a little after five, and I have to go," I stand.

147

"Jack."

"Yeah?"

"Thank you for listening."

"No problem, see you around nine."

"I'll make us dinner," she stands up, walking to the kitchen.

"No, no, just relax. Take a bath, I have bubbles," she smiles, chuckles and returns to the love seat, puts her hands in her lap, her legs pressed together and crossed. I think she somehow magically put on makeup since she stood up. "Enticing ain't it? Make something if you want but don't worry about me."

"Why do you have bubbles?"

"Can't a guy want to treat himself, hmm?" I playfully stormed out hearing a little laughter from behind me. Maybe I'm just hearing what I want to hear again.

I am Leopold von Sacher-Masoch.

**Saturday, 6:20pm, It Was the Wine!**

Yes, yes, yes I know I'm the biggest dick in the world right now. I ruined her life and now am off gallivanting about town, but what would you do? Not keep your appointments. Fuck that. Don't judge me. She made her choices and I feel as though I'm being pretty generous, giving her a place to stay and listening to her problems. I can't be her emotional tampon anymore. I'm just doing what I do, have fun, and yes there may be an element of seriousness added now that she's crashing with me but hey, that's life. Serious shit comes and goes, you can't one-eighty a lifestyle. Hey, come on, don't give me that look. This is my story not hers. Remember that.

Red light: meditate, I must clear my mind; deep breath in deep, breath out. All's well in hell and the angels cry. There is no better feeling than the relaxing pull back of a rapid heartbeat into a slow and powerful thud. God, I could use a smoke. Damn, left them in my other jacket. Green light: slowly I let off the break for the turn, the sound of half a dozen irate motorists honking and swearing breaks my concentration, I stop and throw the car in park. If it isn't one thing it's everything. You know what the horn was invented for, don't you? An old English law stated that any self-propelled vehicle must be preceded by a man on foot carrying a red flag blowing a horn, now that wouldn't fly in todays' fast passed world, would it? Also it just looks fucking ridiculous, so the spectacle was refined to a small horn within the car. Brilliant upgrade I would say. Eventually, it was made standard in most cars. The horn was also an established way of calling for help if your car broke down, or you want to signal a passing cop, or warn the people around of possible danger. Not so some short fused ass hole can voice his frustration at being late for his appointment to Dunkin'. I hate when tools are misused.

Ladies and gentlemen, boys and girls, miscreants of all ages, do not attempt what you're about to see. These are not trained professionals. And of course in the event I get shot or whatever I got you as a witness, right? I open my car door and step out, the honking continues. I bow for my audience. The crowd roars, I best not deny my loyal fans a show. I prepare my speech and quickly stride over to the double-chinned man directly behind me. I hunch to his window and put on my best panic face.

"Sir, are you alright? Do you need any help?" I say in a gasp, trying to through him off.

"What the hell's the matter with you? Go!" he's flailing his arms and shaking his head as he speaks, the flaps and fold in his fat face fly with each turn of the head.

"Do you need any medical assistance?" a cardiologist, perhaps?

"What?" now he's confused.

"Do you need an ambulance?"

"No? Wait, why are you…" his eyes squint as I interrupt.

"Is there any emergency, any one at all?"

"Hey dipshit move your fucking car?" he bats his fingers on the steering wheel repeatedly before thrusting his arms forward towards the direction of my car.

"Are you sure you're ok? You honked your horn."

"Yeah… so you will go…" he really holds on to that 'O'.

"But you honked the horn. You signaled assistance, I would be remised if I did not assist my fellow man in a time of crisis."

"Moron, get the fuck out of the way."

"So you're saying I'm an idiot for mistaking that a person would use a tool designed to signal assistance properly. Well if that ain't the pot calling the kettle an R-tard," he gets out, ooh big boy. He's about five inches taller than me and at least twice my weight.

"Ya'know I'm getting real sick of your shit," he looks down at me, his jowls dangling above my forehead, shaking as he speaks.

"Really, I'm surprised you put up with it for this long," you chinless bastard.

"Now move!" he pushes me, pushes like a schoolyard bully.

"Nah, I think this is more fun," I grab him by the collar, hop up, digging my knees into his enormous gut and… "Ouch!"

always remember no one wins in a head-butt, dumb idea. Well, at least fat fucks nose is broken.

That escalated beautifully, I really need to see V. I need to blow off some steam. Always, always keep sanitizing wipes in the glove compartment: they're great for the cold and flu season, cleaning up ketchup, barbeque sauce, and... blood. Notice the honking stopped almost immediately after I gave my two cents, that's called captivating your audience. You might be wondering if I'm going to get arrested or at least worried that I might. The answer to both is no. There's too much on my plate now for jail, my car is painfully common, the only guy in any position to have seen my plates is hopefully getting his nose reset by now, and sometimes when you really, really, REALLY need it you just get a win once in a while. Plus, I'm almost at Vanessa's complex and haven't been pulled over yet, that's a pretty good sign. I park out front on the street, cops wouldn't expect anyone to be this stupid.

The street is in a fairly decent area, fresh paved roads, good looking sidewalks, the grass is green, and the air doesn't reek of piss, shit or exhaust. If I could pick anywhere else to live in this county it would probably be here.

I enter her building and say 'hi' to Carl the doorman. He knows how to button his trap. He tells me the mister is out and is not to be expected for a while. I tip him for his assistance. It's always easy to tell what mood Vanessa's in, be it romance or in need of a good romp she'll make her point known. Setting foot on her floor I can smell vanilla and lavender, Thelonious's 'Honeysuckle rose' is on the record player. She's prepared a night for us. Sweet Vanessa, what I like about her is that she actually puts effort into making things special.

She doesn't believe in gendered obligations, so if she wants romances she's the one that has to put forth the effort in the affair. I knock on her door 'Shave and a Haircut...Two Bits'. I see a flicker of light through the peephole, the door opens. She smiles and pulls me in pretending like she cares if her neighbors see. We immediately go to the bedroom making out, groping, I sit on the bed looking at her and the room around. She's set it up pretty nice. Look candles, red wine, a California Merlot, two glasses, lights dimmed with a red cloth over the shade. She really knows how to treat a guy.

"So how was your day?" avoiding her asking me first.

"Alright, same old same old," she rips my jacket off.

"Come, come, there's more than that, what held you so long? Parents, wedding plans, a psycho home invader with a hook for a hand holding you hostage, oh no look behind you!" she laughs and calms down a little.

"Well I was with Mike," her fiancé if you didn't already deduce his name was Mike, "and he asked if we were still serious."

"About marriage?" oh boy, did he drop the hammer?

"Yeah, I guess. He asked if I ever thought about seeing other people."

"And what did you say?" she's blushing at me. I better drink, this might be the end of an era.

"I love how things are, and I couldn't possibly see myself with another person."

"Are you ending things here? S'this my send-off fuck?" I refill my glass.

"Where are you getting that from? I said I can't see myself with *another* person. You're still mine. You'll always be," bow-wow.

"Ok, then," phew... that could've been bad.

"I got to change," she kisses me. "Wait for me?"

"'If you're not too long, I'll wait for you all my life.'" Yeah that's right, I went Wilde.

Now, time to really observe. I wish I had her pad; I love the large bay window next to the bed, I don't care if it overlooks the highway. Just to be peacefully woken up by the rising sun would be a nice change of pace over the eight o'clock police sirens I tend to face. The color patterns in this place are seamless, the shade of white or cream that coats the walls blends well with the light brown carpet and both of which are great for reflecting the red of the light. Having this huge bed and the cozy, not small, but cozy kitchen with a stocked pantry would make me oh ever so happy. I've always loved this place. I should come here more often, it's not like it's a hassle and we do on occasion switch it up. But more often than not it's my place we frequent when she's involved.

I'm getting undressed, mmm more wine, wow she really went all out: rose peddles on the bed, smooth jazz and candles are the usual when she's in a romantic mood but looky here at her bureau, right next to the candles, she brought out the sensual oils, a long peacock feather and in the corner of the mirror, with pink and red lipstick she drew a smiley face. She bought a new bedspread, red satin, and white pillow cases with small embroidered hearts overlapping each other. Ohhhh... the bad thing about satin, and with silk, is that it spots if the slightest bit of water gets on it (note to self: never use the good linen in the summer, too much sweat), nineteen drops and two relatively large shadows, the engagement is off. I hope she's not trying to bury her feelings in me. I'm an event not a distraction, and I should be treated as such.

She comes in wearing a red transparent nighty with black feathers at the top and bottom. The feathered bottom rests over her thigh; it's the only form of coverage. Everything is on display; her pubis shaved into a heart. The nighty itself stretched tight over her immaculate bust, straining the fabric, the rest lightly spread over her torso, it blooms outward around her hip and sways with each step she takes, back and forth, back and forth. I'm sorry, am I drooling? Vanessa's black hair spread long draping over her shoulders covering the garments straps; the lingerie looks as if it were just hanging on by her tits.

She's in full makeup: red lipstick, light blush, she highlighted her cheek bones, mascara, eyeshadow that starts purple and transitions to red. Damn, double damn, and something is incredibly wrong. No blood flow. Stall, stall!

"Um... looks like someone's been crying here?"

"Yeah."

"You?" ok still no boner, must be the wine.

"God no, Mike," it has to be the wine.

"Why?"

"Well, I told you that I love how things are," she sprawls out on the bed.

"Yeah?" damn limp dick, don't ruin this. I need some form of stability.

"Then he asked if I was cheating on him, apparently you had left a few hickies on my breasts last time. 'Define cheating,' I inquired and after his simplistic criteria was spouted I told him how long you and I have been together, he broke down. It was a little funny how quiet he gets when angry."

"Is that what you wanted to tell me?"

"Most of it."

"So what's the rest?"

"I'll tell you later. Come on, get in bed," she rolls on all fours.

"Why not now?"

"Reasons."

"Why?" she straightens up on her knees, hand on her hips.

"Because the word abortion isn't sexy," my stomach drops, for a second I feel alone, she said that way too casually.

"What?"

"Yeah, why the hell do you think he'd bawl his eyes out?"

"Well…"

"The cheating? He expected me to say yes, so he was prepared. Confirming his suspicions wouldn't evoke those types of emotions, sure he'd be pissed but I really wanted to drive the hammer home. Don't worry it was his."

"Really?"

"Really, I wouldn't lie to you. Come on hurry, get on the bed while the tears are still wet," fuck that's brutal.

"Ok," we try wrestling but I just can't. She's ball bustingly gorgeous I mean look at those legs, lips, and hips. My tongue may be in her mouth but damn, she would rather a fuck buddy than a family, what the hell man? But how can I judge? There's a beautiful woman alone in my apartment and I'm ignoring her. Fuck me.

"Listen, babe I have an idea," I say, she's laying on top of me. She stops biting my neck, pushes herself up to look at me, her tongue pinched between her teeth.

"Yeah?"

"Want to get a little kinky tonight?"

"What kind of kinky?" she sits up, straddling and starts scratching my ribs, moving her hands closer together, they meet, she lays her palms flat on my chest.

"Back to our roots. Some bondage? A little S&M?" her face lights up.

"I'll get my gear," she hops off of me and runs into the closet with a huge grin. On her knees in front of a chest, she starts naming off all the toys she has, I already know most of them. I walk up behind her while she's holding a riding crop, I've never seen that one before. "Bae, this was my first crop. Here take it," she hands it to me. The leather end is almost serrated from overuse. "It's been a while, I'm surprised you want to do this again."

"I felt we needed a break."

"Why?" she whines.

"I mean, y'know."

"Not really, we kinda just stopped. Why?"

"Cus' I... I don't... because... I don't know. I guess control ain't really my thing."

"So-so-so, now you wanna be my master?" she kisses my nose repeatedly.

"Well, I think I'll make an exception tonight."

"Cus' I've been such a bad *widdle gurl*," speaking in a baby voice while biting her lower lip and still not even a partial, how can this be?

"Yeah."

"Why do you hate being the dom?"

"I don't get a thrill from hitting women."

"Even if she wants you to?" she pulls me in close and starts nibbling on my ear.

"Well, I guess in that case," I lightly tap her ass with the crop, it springs right back. Perfection is possible! "Bend over," she happily does as she's told, leaning on the chest. I whip.

"Oooh, harder," well if you insists. I secure my grip, pull it to my ear and release. Her nails dig into the varnish, chipping some of the laminate. "Ow, not that hard," she chuckles, "well not right now."

"Sorry still getting used to it," I whip again, lighter this time.

"Yeah, just like that," I start tracing my initials on each cheek. Fanning and brushing her asshole with the leather end, she clenches and shivers. I look to my right and see a pair of handcuffs dangling from the doorknob. I change hands with the crop and grab the cuffs.

"On all fours," she complies, lowering herself she runs parallel with the chest shaking her ass. I squeeze the handle, my thumb scratching the textured grip and I whip as hard as I can, knocking her to the floor. She's trembling from the pain but says nothing just biting her lip with closed eyes, smiling. I quickly cuff her.

"Getting really kinky," she's laughing with my hand on the hand on the back of her head, holding her down. "What are you doing honey?"

"I'm not your honey, not your bunny, not your bae, I'm nothing." I am Damocles on the throne of Dionysius, "I'm leaving."

"What are you playing?" she's still smiling, sincerely smiling. I don't understand. I stand outside the closet with the whip in my hand looking down at the pathetic being of depravity rolling on the floor giggling. With her hands cuffed behind her back, she blows the hair from her eyes every few seconds, the jet of air makes a rustling noise as it blows past her nose. Enjoy your kink but don't bind your heart. She still thinks I'm playing.

"No games. I'm done."

"No you're not, this is too much fun," I turn away. "Look at me. Look at me!" I do. I drop to my knees looking her dead in the eyes.

"Vanessa, I'm gone, out. *Ragazza, io sono finito a ti.*"

"Why?" she seems so sad, the tone of her voice is languid and weak.

"Cus' this isn't real."

"What?"

"I mean this isn't real enough for me anymore. Sorry about that, when I have these conversations usually the other party can read my mind," she looks at me like I'm crazy. "I have to move on," I stand up and drop the riding crop.

"Jack."

"Shut up, for once. Just… shut… up."

"I love you," my heart stops, fuck you.

"Don't do that."

"I do."

"No, you don't. You think we belong together, that-that-that we're the same or something."

"Aren't we?"

"No, not today. A few days ago, yeah, sure you would have been right. You would have been my bride in bondage but times change."

"What changed?" I closed the closet door, I can't look anymore.

As I'm gathering my clothes she's not screaming or cussing my name but weeping quietly, I can hear each gentle moan and sob. The panting of that miserable girl is ripping me to shreds. I'm beginning to feel faint. Pretty soon there'll be nothing left but a purple shirt, leather shoes, black pants and a jacket collapsed on her floor. I want to leave as quickly as possible, but there's something stopping me, some force that's driving me to stay here and endure this decomposition. I'm sitting on her bed in my boxers staring at the closet, the record has begun to skip and that second is played over and over again. I am frozen in those notes. The needle screeches and jumps halfway through the song. I can now continue. I put on my pants and pause for a moment rifling through my pockets, fondling my spare change. I take out five dollars and thirty-eight cents and put it on her bedside table.

I continue forcing the rest of my clothes on for what must have been forty-five minutes. The record had ended, and I'm just left with silence. She had stopped crying within that time and has stayed silent. I can't stand that buzzing when a room's too quiet, it's driving me mad. There's a wasps nest in my head, and they're getting more irritated with each passing second. "Stop it," I yell hoping to break the silence and give me peace, if only for a second. Vanessa doesn't make a noise. I don't know why she doesn't use the safety-release on the cuffs, come out of the closet and yell at me, give me something. I want some noise to end this horrible silence, something that isn't just me yelling at open space like a mad man, please Vanessa if you do love me then hate me. I'm finish dressing and ready to leave without saying another word, but I guess I should undo her cuffs. I walk back to the closet and open it.

"It's a little funny, y'know. When I was a kid, I would hide things I was ashamed of in the back of my closet."

"What the fuck kind of response is that! You dump me and throw me in here, and that's what you have to say, the fucks the matter with you!"

"Let's be fair, I threw you in the closet before I dumped you."

"Like it matters."

"Look on the bright side I usually bury my problems, granted they're emotional but still you have to admit this is a little better. Come on, let me take off those cuffs."

"They've been off since you closed the door."

"Oh," I'm not surprised.

"How do you not see that?"

"I guess I was looking at your eyes," she gets a little quiet and breaks eye contact.

"That's a bit sentimental," she mumbles.

"I never said I didn't have fond feelings for you."

"I beg to differ."

"I looked forward to seeing you, I always have. As close as I can love you without violating the terms of our relation I did. I do. But we both know you belong with someone else, and I'm just getting in the way, a bad habit."

"Jack," she sits up on her knees.

"It's fine. Something I've come to terms with, I am what I am. I-I just don't want to do any more damage."

"I was sincere Jack, I do love you."

"That'd be great if I loved you," I cross my arms and lean on the frame, my shadow absorbs her in the small box. There's a glimmer of light shining through her tears.

"And you can't because of rule three."

"The dreaded rule three," I smile at her.

"So you do care about me?" she jumps; excited and sad.

"Yes, but I just can't do this anymore. You could've been happy with your guy. You would have been happy if you just pushed me away when someone loved you. I'm doing this not to save you, not to stop any feelings I may have or had for you. I, as selfish as I can be, am doing what you should have done a long time ago so I may be able to finally be happy and avoid the same mistakes you keep making. If we continue with our arrangement it'll just be that, an arrangement. Yes, we might have some good times and I might grow to love you but do you really want me to have to try to love you?"

"It's better than you leaving," she reaches out to me, her hand quivering.

"No, no it's not," I help her up. "Ciao bella," I give her a kiss on the cheek and she bursts into tears, may Mike know retribution. I run to my car. A part of me is in that apartment: a part of my soul, my time, I gave a portion of my life to be buried in that little one bed one bath, and I hope she takes good care of it. I might have loved her a little. After I take my minute to look back at all the happy memories I had in that room or just with that girl, I get in my car.

**Saturday, 7:45pm, Redemption**

Barreling off exits like a demon that just clawed his way out of hell, I am Asmodeus ready to stick my fangs deep into the veins of temptation. The shimmering red, yellow and white eyes of the other unwanted creatures glazed on the black pavement light my way home. The odometer tickles ninety-five twice before I realized I've been going above eighty. The rumbling of the engine shakes throughout my body like the infernal winds that have taken so many other wantons. I press on the breaks as Stevie Ray Vaughan's *'Cold Shot'* blasts out of my speakers letting the patron around know 'I am here.'

My minds racing; faster and faster, I'm in a panic. Oh that's new, I haven't felt this in a long time. It's like having your first kiss or losing you virginity or being pegged for the first time, you don't know what to expect but you're excited. I can't wait to see Rachel, I know exactly what I have to do. Shit that sounds cheesy, I might have lied a little in the beginning saying 'this is my life, not a romance story' but who's to say that there can't be a little romance in life, especially mine. Everything has some aspect of romance in it, from seduction and seclusion to the destruction of the world. When I have a girl all to myself I try to make it us and us alone, it's magic when you feel like you're the only two left. Is that not what romance is?

I screwed up big time abandoning Rachel when she needed me, and I fucking promised I'd never do that. I shouldn't have done that, or am I abandoning Vanessa right now? It doesn't matter Vanessa's crazy, Rachel is the one I want; she's the one who needs me. And I need her. I don't know if I believe in fate or God or any of that crap but I do know I was happiest with her in my life and maybe I should tell her that, I should've told her that.

My parking is a disaster, on the curb and almost took out a fire hydrant. Dings and scratches are nothing, not at this moment. Nothing matters, not even the mustang whose mirror I just smashed. No time to write a note. What do you do in this situation key 'sorry' in their door? I walk onto the sidewalk, lock my car fondling my keys. As I step closer to my building, I can hear the scurrying of the rats and addicts running deep into the darkness, and I'm not repulsed.

The sky is beginning to take on a gold and purple hue, perfect. I run up the stairs to the second floor, down my hall, finally at my door. My heart is about to explode.

"Rachel," knocking on the door "Rachel," wait why am I knocking on my own door, forget about the idiocy, it's more dramatic this anyway "Rachel!" she opens the door.

"How shit faced are you?" no makeup on, dressed in a ratty old sweater and a pair of my boxers, her hair's wet and arms crossed, and yet she's still adorable. I must be in love.

"What, what are you saying?"

"That's the only explanation for why you, lord of this manor, who drove so I know you have your keys, would rather stand outside the door yelling my name like an idiot than open the door yourself." She sniffs my breath, "wine, who gets drunk on wine?" is that the green eyed monster I see peering out?

"I'm not drunk. I just thought… uh… knocking seemed more dramatic, anyway, can we sit I have something to say."

"Be my guest," she stepped back and waves me through.

I took her by the hand and walked to the love seat, "Rachel, this is gonna sound crazy, and I know it's crazy, but I love you." I pause and look down, my hands are shaking, "my fucked up life is just the wake of the damage caused by your leaving. I loved you then, I love you now, and I tried to forget, I tried to forget you, forget how good it felt to feel for someone. I tried to forget by fucking anything that'd take me but I can't anymore, I just can't. Shit this is corny, but I don't know how to say it without sounding like a rom-com rip off."

"Oh, Jack my dear I feel the same…" Too much? I can't write a good ending to this story, and you know I've tried. I just wanted to impress you. I'm sorry for lying so much…

**Friday, 6:25 am Served… Back to Reality in Fall River**

"I don't have to do anything, good bye Johnny boy."

And that's it, to the only person whose opinion ever mattered to me. In one day she became the most important person in my life, and you know what? She doesn't even want to hear my bull-shit. She had no interest in me, pulling me over was just a coincidence. And this… I guess she just wanted me out of her life for good and didn't have the nerve to say it aloud. I don't blame her for a moment, all she did was to say 'hey' thought maybe catch up with an old friend, see how much we've changed and within a day I… I couldn't even hide how fucked up I am for a day, cut out the tumor before the cancer spreads. I get it.

This ain't the first time I've been rejected and I know it won't be the last, but she, Rachel, is always going to be the one that I'll remember dearly, explicitly, painfully. 'Here's to looking at you, kid,' God fucking damn it Bogey. I know I'm a coldhearted bastard, you know it, but I can't deal with losing Rachel like this, it must help if you go out looking like a hero, it must. At least you can say you did the right thing and as you can see I have never been an advocate for that. Even in my fantasies I'm an asshole. So what did I do when I met an old buddy? I fucking used her and worse of all any fond memories or feelings she may have or had are now tainted by whatever she saw on those tapes; the dark accumulation of the shit that I am concentrated into one suppressed moment. I don't even want to see that vile beast.

The real story, if you care to hear, ends with her getting all charges dropped and driving me here. We get into an argument and she storms out, leaving me without a way home. I pulled out my pocket diary once she left and started this farce. I still don't know how she got me out and probably never will. I'm content with not knowing. I'll never see her again I can tell you that much and I accept it, I mean why would anyone want any form of relationship with such a lowly individual like myself? I have failed at being a friend, a good brother and a real man. I have alienated every prospect I've had and who very well could have been the way to a real and healthy relationship, but I'm incapable of that, we both know it. I couldn't even persuade an old friend, someone who I shared everything with when I was a kid, to stay for ten fucking minutes. I'm so fucking lonely. I need a smoke. I pull out my cigarettes, light and puff.

"Hey, hey you can't do that," the busboy drops the broom and runs up to me; yes I know it's illegal but fuck off I need one.

"Nobody's here kid. I know it's been outlawed for like ever, but I just need a break man. After the day I've had, come on?" rational brain working.

"It's still not allowed, please put it out," he tries to grab it out of my hand. I stand and bang my palm on the table.

"I just got out of jail, I ain't afraid of going back for jamming this butt in your fucking eye," the waitress runs up to us.

"Hey, hey everyone settle down," I plop down in the booth looking down and take another puff.

"He's smoking," the little fink rats me out like the fucker he is. How blind is this bitch for him to have to tell?

"It's ok Sam, let it go," I sit silent like a child between arguing parents.

"But... but..." she put her hands on his shoulders, kid just listen to the old bitty.

"Let it go, he's not hurting anyone."

"Yet," I give my two cents, the waitress gives me the evil eye.

"Go sweep over there if it bothers you so much."

"Yes ma'am."

"Punk ass," again I give my thoughts.

"He's just a kid."

"And a fink."

"You best finish up your coffee and get out," she walks away.

"Yeah, yeah," I throw my cigarette at the window across the walkway, the kid looks over at it, then at me. I stare him down as I sip my coffee. He looks away.

Where was I? Oh yeah, I wouldn't have cared if she believed me or even wanted her to really listen, but to have sat and pretend that what I had to say mattered for a little while would have changed the entire tone of this good bye. She could have at least let me keep my sanity. I massage my temples, I hear whispers. I can hear Shawn in the back of my head, his voice growing louder than all the others. It's Shawn to the rescue. He has this power that no matter how screwed one may feel he can comfort them. That's why I need him now. He comes from the living ember of my discarded cigarette, his boot smothers the red ash and he sits in front of me.

"If it ain't broke too bad don't throw it away, isn't that what your dad always said?"

"I don't know, maybe."

"Where did you hear that then?"

"I don't know I was young, I guess it was my dad."

"Where'd he say it?"

"*Je ne sais pas.*"

"In the garage? While working on the car?"

"Maybe."

"On the wrecked family car, after mother-may-I was in hospice, the car she crashed. Do you really think he meant the car?"

"What else could he mean?" I am so pissed right now, stop just stop thinking. Please fade away.

"Well…" The pain is back, cutting into my thoughts I can't even keep a clear image of him anymore.

"Don't you dare, don't fucking say it. My mom was not broken!" I have to have a brain tumor or something, this isn't right.

"They're your thoughts, Jack you're hurting. Go ahead text her, you deserve it. You need a little something to take your mind off of tonight," Shawn fades away. But that voice lingers, the tone and words telling me 'I need a release' I want one, I want the pain gone. I want everything. I go straight to my opiate. I pull out my phone, I scroll through my contacts and select her. She'll understand. I think heavily on what to say. How can I start a good conversation? I don't want to come off desperate, but I can't sound cold. I need her, after filing through all possibilities I decide and start texting:

*Siobhan?*

*I'm here*

*What are you up to?* It is composed so beautifully; simple, interested and above all nonchalant.

*NM, you??* An immediate response, a tear drops on my screen. Thank you.

*Just got released and I'm feeling a little lonely* play it cool and she's yours.

*Aw, honey. He's in the shower, I'll be free in half an hour if you really miss me*

*You have no idea,* ok cool it, don't need to sound needy.

*Really?;-\**

*For reals*

*I'm sorry I couldn't help earlier, i was just frustrated and worried he might find out. Please forgive me*

*I can never be mad at you ;-\**

*Is it tru what they say about men fresh out of prison, they go at it like animals?*

*Wouldn't you like to find out :-P*

*☺☺☺YAS, so when may I expect you?*

God damn it, I hate myself. I'm in too deep to change, and know what? It works for me. How sick am I that insincerity and superficiality are what suits me? Rachel leaves and almost instantly I go after someone else, someone to help kill my pain. I want to throw this God damn phone through that window and cut off my supply and be something else. But I can't just leave them, any of them, I am Providence and I can't forsake my disciples. I want to send *in an hour* I'm probably going to, the blood starts rushing south. This is how the world works and for that I deserve to be in this social Elba. Vive le France!

I am reminded, be it the emptiness I feel in this moment or maybe I'm just getting nostalgic, of the last time I slept with Erin, João's mistress. Looking back I think she knew it was the last time. We talked for about an hour before and after. Why do we exist? Why do we do what we do? Existentialism was our topic of discussion for the night. She submitted to concepts similar to that Kierkegaard and Sartre in her saying we establish our own meaning in life while I took an absurdist even cosmic nihilist perspective. She said, "we live, we love, we die and we are comforted by the memories of what had made us happy and say to the young with our last breath 'This is what life is,'" I kissed her told her it's a nice though.

To her theory, I responded with "life is short and sweet with just enough pain and suffering to make it interesting. It is the longest and most difficult thing that I have ever had the pleasure to endure." I meant it as a joke but she took an air of seriousness not talking after I said it, I felt I did something wrong. We held hands and she began to cry. I asked her if she was alright, she never answered. She knew. She had to have known.

I hear footsteps approaching, I dare not look up at the judging eyes of the waitress or whoever telling me to leave. She sits down.

"Ok Jack, you have five minutes."

Then again, my friend, I have been wrong before...

www.ingramcontent.com/pod-product-compliance
Lightning Source LLC
Chambersburg PA
CBHW021010180626
46814CB00003B/1223